I0610030

Thomas Radford

Observations on the Caesarean Section and on Other

Obstetric Operations

With an appendix of cases

Thomas Radford

Observations on the Caesarean Section and on Other Obstetric Operations
With an appendix of cases

ISBN/EAN: 9783337411169

Printed in Europe, USA, Canada, Australia, Japan

Cover: Foto ©Andreas Hilbeck / pixelio.de

More available books at **www.hansebooks.com**

OBSERVATIONS

ON THE

CÆSAREAN SECTION

AND ON

OTHER OBSTETRIC OPERATIONS.

With an Appendix of Cases.

BY

THOMAS RADFORD, M.D.,

F.R.C.P.EDIN., F.R.C.S.ENG., ETC.,

HONORARY CONSULTING PHYSICIAN TO ST. MARY'S HOSPITAL,
MANCHESTER.

MANCHESTER.

———

MDCCCLXV.

CONTENTS.

INTRODUCTORY REMARKS.

THE Cæsarean section is not an operation of recent date; its performance is recorded before obstetric medicine and surgery were scientifically accepted (vide *Edinburgh Medical and Surgical Journal*, vol. xxv), and has since been generally recognised in most of the modern systems of obstetricy. Although this is the fact, yet it has not received the unanimous approval of the members of our profession. From a very early date it has had its advocates and its opponents. To my knowledge, there has been no subject connected with medicine which has created more bitterness of feeling and animosity in the minds of those who may be classed as Cæsareanists and anti-Cæsareanists.

In no city or town in these empires have these repugnant and unprofessional feelings existed to a greater extent than in Manchester. The important but rancorous controversy which took place here between Dr. Hull and Mr. Simmons brought the greater part of the medical profession to entertain more clear and definite opinions. The writings of Dr. Hull, apart from their controversial character, contain most valuable and practical observations.

When I received the honour of appointment to deliver the first obstetric address before the Provincial (now named British) Medical Association, at the next meeting which was to take place at Manchester, I selected a practical and at that time a debateable subject; and, even at the present time, the opinions of medical men are unsettled and discordant upon it. My opinions upon some parts of the subject, no doubt, differed from the great majority of those who honoured me by patiently listening to its delivery; yet I did not hesitate freely, and I hope conscientiously, to express them. At the present time, I do not shrink from the responsibility of again bringing more fully before the entire profession my views, which had only been partially known for several years before the delivery of the address. I have the fullest confidence that the doctrines

B

promulgated will receive the unprejudiced judgment of the profession.

I was induced to select for my subject the Cæsarean section, and
those other means which have been recommended to supersede its
performance, partly because these subjects have been, as already
stated, warmly discussed in this city; and partly because the greatest
number of cases (I speak relatively) in which the Cæsarean operation
has been performed in Great Britain and Ireland, have occurred in
this city and in the neighbouring districts. The analytical tables
contain a report of seventy-seven cases. Of this number, fifty-five
have happened in England; of which, twenty-five have occurred in
Lancashire; fifteen cases have occurred in Scotland; and seven cases
have taken place in Ireland. It is a remarkable fact, that there
stands no case recorded from Wales.

The following observations are entirely confined to British and
Irish cases. I have purposely avoided admitting foreign cases into
the tables, or of making remarks upon, or of drawing any deductions
from them; although I am quite aware the maternal mortality might
be shown to be considerably less by their admission for computation, than it appears by only taking the results of British and Irish
practice.

In the following pages, all the questions have been faithfully and
conscientiously discussed; and all the opinions which are given are,
as far as possible, based on facts. My object is to endeavour to place
the Cæsarean section, and some other obstetric operations, on such
medical, social, and moral grounds, as to be approved by both the
profession and society at large. The doctrines which I have inculcated in the following pages are only desired to be received in the
spirit in which they have been written; and I desire them to be
taken in no other way than as they are worthy of acceptance or
rejection.

The tables which were brought before the Association contained
records of many points which have been now omitted in order to
reduce them. They contained an account of the number of previous
labours, and the mode of delivery; the state, etc., of the os uteri;
the location of the placenta, etc.; the exact line of the incision; and
some general remarks on the condition of the patient before, during,
and after the operation, etc. I have, however, embodied the deductions to be drawn from the record on most of the subjects above
adverted to.

CHAPTER I.

On the Necessity of the Cæsarean Section as an Obstetric Operation.

IN an ill directed controversial ardour, Mr. Simmons, in his remarks addressed to Dr. Hull, declared that the Cæsarean section was universally and inevitably fatal, and proposed a compound operation of symphyseotomy and craniotomy to supersede it. It was not long afterwards before he had an opportunity of putting in practice his highly lauded operation. He was consulted in the notable case of Elizabeth Thompson, whose pelvis (now in my possession) is extremely distorted. An examination of it must have brought conviction to his mind that some other means must be adopted in order to deliver her. It is to be presumed he renounced his proposed operation, as he discarded his patient, who was afterwards brought to the Manchester Lying-in Hospital, and delivered by the Cæsarean section.

Dr. Hull, at this time, endeavoured to settle the disputed question of the necessity of this operation; and the soundness and justice of his opinions were generally approved of by the profession. If this question had still remained undisturbed, it would have been unnecessary for me to interfere with this part of the subject. Within a few years, however, not only the necessity, but likewise the propriety, of its performance has been denied, and opprobrious epithets employed (unworthy of the talented physician who used them), which, although totally unfounded, not only cast odium on the operation, but also reflect most unjustly on the character of those obstetricians who have conscientiously recommended it and boldly performed it. More recently, it has been declared by an obstetric physician, that the induction of abortion, the induction of premature labour, craniotomy, or these two last operations combined and applied according to the degree of distortion, would render the Cæsarean section altogether unnecessary.

The Cæsarean section is doubtless required whenever the pelvic apertures, or its cavity, are so diminished that a mutilated infant cannot possibly be drawn through. This diminution may be positively produced when the pelvic bones are distorted by mollities ossium, by rickets, or by irregular union of, or by a large deposition of callus on, these bones after fractures; or from exostosis, which may grow upon any portion of the bones.

The pelvis is also sometimes relatively so diminished by different kinds of large tumours which are lodged within its cavity; some of which are loose, whilst others are immoveably fixed so as to render this operation necessary.

An analytical statement of the causes which have rendered the performance of the Cæsarean section necessary in these kingdoms, will be found numerically to stand as follows. Of the seventy-seven tabulated cases, forty-three were produced by mollities ossium, of which thirty-two were English, ten Scotch, and one Irish. In fourteen cases, the pelvis was distorted from rickets, of which twelve were English and two Scotch.

In one case, the distortion was congenital (English), and was of a rickety character; in two cases, one English and one Scotch, the pelvis had been fractured.

In six cases, fibrous or other tumours existed in the pelvis; of which three were English, two Scotch, and one Irish. In two cases, there was an exostosis growing from the base of the sacrum; of which one was English and one Irish. In two English cases, carcinoma of the os and cervix uteri caused the obstruction. In seven cases, the cause is not recorded.

Nearly all the pathological causes enumerated above which render the Cæsarean section necessary are progressive; and most of them may proceed to such an extent as nearly to obliterate the apertures of the pelvis, or to block up the cavity.

I have in my possession, a distorted pelvis in which the brim is nearly destroyed, there not being a greater space between the descending lumbar vertebræ and the pubes on each side than the tenth part of an inch. The space between the lumbar vertebræ and the rami of the pubes is five-sixteenths of an inch, and the space between the jutting of the pubes near the symphysis is three-eighths of an inch.

So, likewise, exostosis, or tumours within the cavity, have grown so large as to prevent a finger from passing without great difficulty.

These pelvic conditions may exist in a first pregnancy, or may come on at any time during the child-bearing period; and a woman who has had several natural and propitious labours may, in successive cases, have greater or less impediments existing, which may require different means for her delivery; or the pelvis may be naturally capacious in one labour, and in her next the bones may be so distorted, or its cavities may be so filled, as to require the Cæsarean section.

Then, with such uncertainties as these, it is obvious that both the patient and practitioner may be completely ignorant of these organic conditions until pregnancy has either been considerably advanced, or even completed, and labour commenced.

Surely, the most benighted opponent to the Cæsarean section cannot be so mentally blind as not to know that young married women can not be compelled to submit to vaginal or other examinations in order that it may be ascertained whether there is sufficient pelvic capacity for a full-grown infant to pass through. But, supposing the practitioner to be acquainted with the state of the pelvis, the means recommended to supersede the performance of the Cæsarean section are quite inadequate to prevent its necessity in those higher states of distortion, etc., which have existed in most, if not all, of the cases which are tabulated. Ample testimony exists of the truth of the above remark in some of the cases contained in the tables.

Dr. Hull relates several cases, and within my own knowledge others have occurred, in which it was quite impossible to deliver the women after either embryotomy or craniotomy had been performed. Then, under these circumstances, what measures must be adopted for the delivery of the woman? Must she die undelivered with a mangled infant still in the womb? This event has been most unwarrantably allowed to happen. Again, ought the Cæsarean section to be performed to extract a mutilated infant? This practice has been pursued. These are weighty reasons why the Cæsarean operation should be considered as one, at least, of necessity. There are, however, other grounds to be spoken of, which further establish this proposition. No doubt every obstetrician will admit that it is absolutely necessary for the os uteri to be accessible when he intends to induce abortion; more especially, if this operation is to be performed by the aid of instruments. And when, at later periods of pregnancy, craniotomy is contemplated, it would doubtless be con-

sidered a *sine quâ non* that both the os uteri, the degree of its dilatation, and also that the presentation of the infant, should be ascertained before this destructive operation is performed. These important desiderata do not, however, always exist in cases in which the
pelves are highly distorted.

In twenty-one of the tabulated cases, the os uteri could not be
felt ; in twenty-one cases there is no account given, from which it is
fair to conclude that it could not be touched—making together
forty-two cases. In thirty-five cases, the os uteri was discovered
with more or less difficulty. In sixteen cases, no part of the infant
could be reached. In forty-one cases, we have no account ; which
omission affords negative or presumptive evidence that the presentation could not be ascertained, which together make fifty-seven
cases. In twenty-one cases, the following presentations are recorded :
in twelve the head, in three the hand, in two a hand and a foot, in
one a foot, in one a hip, and in two the arms.

The foregoing remarks, and the above authenticated facts, are,
I hope, amply sufficient to establish the proposition of the necessity
of the Cæsarean section as a recognised obstetric operation. Although
the subsequent observations do not relate to the necessity of the
operation, yet I deem them so practically important that I have
ventured to place them in this chapter.

In some cases of rupture of the uterus, the infant might be removed with more safety to the mother by an abdominal section, than
by dragging it away either by the feet or by the crotchet. Trask's
extensive statistics are very favourable to its adoption in some cases
of this accident.

When a woman who is nearly at the full period of pregnancy dies,
or if killed by accident, the obstetrician is, morally, socially, and
professionally, bound to propose *post mortem* hysterotomy. Justice
to the incarcerated (most likely living) infant demands an immediate
decision, as too long delay would be hazardous to its life. It is,
however, a well known fact, that the infant survives the death of its
mother much longer than is usually supposed. In this empire, medical men are quite at liberty to exercise a free and conscientious
judgment ; they are not trammeled by theological dogmas, as they
are in France and other countries.

CHAPTER II.

On the Statistics of the Cæsarean Section.

THE statistics of the results of the Cæsarean section, especially as concerns the mothers, are highly unfavourable. The general account stands as follows of the seventy-seven women whose cases are tabulated. Sixty-six, or 85.71 per cent., died; eleven, or 14.28 per cent., were saved.

The number of successful cases here mentioned is greater than is usually allowed to have taken place; and, therefore, this statement requires further explanation. They are registered as follows. Nos. 1, 12, 35, 36, 37, 49, 53, 57, 67, 68, and 71; of these, Nos. 1, 12, 36, 49, 53, 67, 68, and 71, perfectly and permanently recovered. Case No. 35—She also recovered; the wounds being nearly healed. She lived several weeks; but afterwards she died from epilepsy, to which malady she had been previously subject. Case No. 37—The woman recovered; and afterwards died from disease of the hip-joint.

There is, however, another case included in the deaths which ought, in my opinion, to be in some measure considered as one of recovery. She lived seven days; and so long as she was rationally treated, she went on favourably. But after the treatment had been injudiciously changed, she gradually grew worse and died.

The special statistics, or the results, of the cases in which I have been concerned are as follows. Of six women, four died, or 66.66 per cent.; and two were saved, or 33.33 per cent.

From the seventy-seven women, seventy-eight infants were extracted; one being a case of twins. Of which forty-six, or 58.97 per cent., were saved; and thirty-two, or 41.02 per cent., were dead. Nearly all these infants were dead before the operation, which might have been saved if it had been earlier performed.

The special statistics, or the number of deaths, in my practice

stand thus.   Of six infants extracted, three, or 50 per cent., were
saved; and three, or 50 per cent., were dead.   Two of this number
were dead before the operation, one of which was putrid; the death
of the other was doubtless chargeable to the operation, and was
caused by a spasmodic seizure of its neck by the uterus during its
extraction.

The risk to infants in Cæsarean births is not much greater than
that which is contingent on natural labours, provided correct principles of practice are adopted.

If I dare venture to give an ideal comparative estimate, I should
say, if it is supposed 1 per cent. be the mortality of natural labour,
that consequent on the Cæsarean section may be stated as scarcely
1½ per cent.

CHAPTER III.

On the Maternal and Infantile Mortality.

HAVING, in the preceding chapter, placed before my readers a full and trustworthy statistical account of the results of the Cæsarean section in the cases in which this operation has been performed in Great Britain and Ireland, I shall next endeavour to prove what the causes are which have occasioned such a fearful fatality of the mothers, and how far they unavoidably belong to the operation. I shall then speak of the infantile deaths and their causes.

To satisfactorily and faithfully accomplish this investigation, the mind ought to be free from all partiality in favour of the Cæsarean section and from all prejudice against it. The deductions on which we seek to establish practical principles ought, as far as possible, to be drawn from well established facts. However true this rule in general is, there is more or less difficulty in strictly observing it on the subject now under our consideration. Most of the cases, in my humble judgment, have been related more for the object of swelling the already fatal list, than for the purpose of pointing out the mischief which existed previously to the operation, and the real causes of death.

I.—*On the Causes of Maternal Mortality.* The constitutional state of most of the women who underwent this operation, was very unfavourable for its performance. Forty-five of them laboured under progressive and incurable disease; many of them were bedridden, and were also unable to discharge their social duties. Many others wanted that perfect or conservative constitutional power to enable them to bear without danger so important an operation.

In most of these cases, the practitioner was ignorant of their nature until his assistance was required during labour, and therefore he could not adopt preparatory measures. In all capital operations, the

risk is greatly enhanced if such means have been neglected. The
blood must be depraved in such subjects, and consequently the
secretions and excretions must be unhealthy; hence the necessity
of taking such steps as tend to correct organic or functional de-
rangement. Constipation is nearly an invariable attendant on ordinary pregnancy ; and, in many cases, fæcal accumulations to a great
amount occur. But when distortion of the pelvis exists, this is
much more likely to happen, in consequence of the mechanical impediment offered by the great projection of the promontory of the
sacrum and lower lumbar vertebræ to the downward passage of the
fæces. The cervical and oral portions of the uterus, which are thrown
backwards against this osseous mass, tend to compress the inter-
vening gut. The same effects, to a greater or less degree, are produced when large tumours exist in the pelvis. The numerous evils
which arise from neglected bowels are not only experienced during
pregnancy, but also during the puerperal state. Such are peritoneal
inflammation, puerperal irritation and exhaustion, etc. If, then,
such serious diseases occur during the puerperal state after ordinary
labours, from causes which are remediable, is it not very probable
that the same mischief might happen after Cæsarean cases, in which
these causes do exist in a still higher degree ?

Labour, if unduly protracted, is nearly always attended and followed by a considerable number of very serious evils.

These mischievous effects vary considerably according to the duration of the labour—to the nature of the cause and the degree of
the mechanical impediment which obstructs the passage of the child
through the pelvis. And, therefore, it is obvious, different measures
must be adopted according to the relative degree of obstruction.
We ought, however, always to consider a lengthened duration of
labour, from whatever cause it arises, as more or less unfavourable
to both the mother and her infant. In all such cases, we should
be extremely watchful, and timely adopt those measures relatively
required for the delivery of the woman before any injury is inflicted
on, or irreparable mischief is done to, the pelvic tissues or organs.
It must be understood, that all the dangers of protraction increase
after the rupture of the membranes and the discharge of the liquor
amnii. It is also a well established fact, that the dangers both to
the mother and to the infant increase in a ratio proportionate to the
duration of labour. I soon learned, from my hospital practice, that
the rules laid down by systematic writers on midwifery, on the treatment of protracted labour, were most mischievous.

To the students of my class, I invariably and urgently inculcated the necessity of an early performance of all obstetric operations, either manual or instrumental, as being of the highest importance, and as especially tending to save the lives of both mother and infant when those instruments were used which are compatible with its life.

In the year 1843, I delivered a short course of lectures to many members of our profession, in which I urged the propriety of an early performance of all obstetric operations, especially of the Cæsarean section; and pointed out the progressive dangers of protraction. At this time, I had no tables to guide my opinion, with the exception of those of Dr. Breen in his observations on the management of tedious labour. (*Edin. Med. and Surg. Journal*, vol. xv, p. 161.) These tables clearly show that dangers increase with the duration of labour. Since this period, Professor Simpson has most satisfactorily proved this fact. It may not, perhaps, be considered irrelevant briefly to mention the effects of labour when unduly and unwarrantably prolonged, in order that a comparison may be made between them and those which have been found existing after the Cæsarean section, and which have been most unjustly attributed to this operation.

Sometimes febrile excitement occurs, accompanied with a quick pulse, hot skin, great thirst, and furred tongue. If means of relief be not afforded, more alarming symptoms soon follow. The tongue becomes covered with sordes; the pulse becomes more feeble; and sinking and exhaustion take place, followed by death. Apoplexy, or hæmorrhage from the lungs, may occur in women predisposed to these diseases; or the large vessels of the heart may suffer. Atony of the uterus happens, giving rise to flooding. Active or sudden rupture of the uterus frequently happens. There often takes place a destruction of tissue in the cervix uteri, from the contusion which this part sustains by the forcible pressure of the child's head against the pelvic bones. The os uteri is sometimes separated from the cervix. In other cases, gangrene of the cervix and os has taken place. Inflammation of the cellular tissue of the pelvis occurs, with its consequent infiltration, suppuration, and abscess. At other times, the textures of the different pelvic organs are destroyed, and sloughing takes place, which makes intercommunications between the vagina and the rectum, or between the vagina and the bladder, constituting recto-vaginal or vesico-vaginal fistula, with a train of evils which make the life of the woman most miserable.

The nervous system may be considerably influenced by the Cæsarean section, as it is by most, if not all, other capital operations, the effect of which is termed "shock". This has been asserted to be a frequent, an unavoidable, and an uncontrollable cause of the woman's death. If an abstract view only be taken of the condition of the patient after the operation, then this statement would in some measure appear to be true. But a careful consideration of all the preceding contingent circumstances which existed in each of the recorded cases, and more especially of those which have occurred to myself, leads me to a different conclusion. All the patients, in whose cases I have been concerned, bore the operation with great fortitude and moral courage; and some of them expressed themselves as having endured less pain than they had felt from one of the labour-throes. There was not any manifestation of shock produced by the operation, which did not exist before its performance. If women who had not been endangered by previous disease, or who had not suffered from the effects of protracted labour, died suddenly, or in a few hours, after this operation, without any rally, then it would be reasonable—nay, quite right—to attribute their deaths to the shock occasioned by it. But the fact is otherwise, as nearly all those patients registered in the tables laboured under an incurable disease, and had been a considerable time in labour. I here insert the durations of the labours in sixteen of the tabulated cases, in which sinking, exhaustion, or the effects of shock, are stated as the real cause of death. In one, it was twelve days; in one, it was ten days; in one, it was seven days; in one, it was six days; in one, it was four to five days (in this case, turning had been unsuccessfully attempted, and afterwards craniotomy ineffectually performed, during which operation the vagina was lacerated); in one, it was a hundred and two hours; in one case, it was three days and a half; in three cases, it was three days (one of these women died from disease of the lungs); in one, it was sixty to seventy hours; in one, it was sixty hours; in one, it was thirty-six to forty hours; in one, it was thirty-five hours; in one, it was thirty-four hours; in one, it was twenty hours. One was only twelve hours in labour. She was greatly reduced in vital power by unavoidable hæmorrhage (placenta prævia); she had also bronchitis and epileptic convulsions both before and after the operation.

These cases require no further comment, than to say they afford sufficient evidence of the real cause of death, which truly cannot be attributed to the operation.

Hæmorrhage with shock is stated to have been the cause of death in some of the tabulated cases. The duration of labour in these women is noted as follows. In one, it was fifty-four hours; in one, fifty-five hours; in one, fifty-six hours; in one, seventy-two hours; in one, thirty hours. In this case, there had been a considerable loss of blood before the operation; but very little was lost afterwards. Embryotomy had been unsuccessfully performed, the uterus ruptured, and the os separated from the cervix uteri. In one case, the labour lasted eighteen hours. There was very little blood lost during the operation; but internal hæmorrhage afterwards took place. There were three pints of blood found.

Hæmorrhage has been alleged to be one of the causes of the fatality of this operation. Dr. Hull, however, in two or three parts of his controversial writings, denies that serious danger occurs from this cause; but a strict analytical inquiry of the tabulated cases proves that this assertion is not correct, but that a greater or less quantity of blood is sometimes lost. In several instances, the discharge was considerable, and perhaps may be said to have been dangerous. The peculiar sources whence blood issues during this operation are from the incised edges of the abdominal and uterine parietes; and, when the placenta is in the way of the incision, it may be cut, and then blood issues from its divided structure. Hæmorrhage sometimes proceeds from the uterine arteries, and from the large sinous openings, and also from the surface of the placenta when it is partially separated; and, when this organ is torn, blood is discharged from its disrupted textures, as happens after ordinary labour. In the seventy-seven cases, it is recorded that in twenty there was no blood lost; in twenty-four, very little was discharged, varying from two to seven ounces in quantity; in five cases, there were seven to ten or twelve ounces; in four cases, there were fourteen to twenty-four ounces discharged. In twelve cases, the extent of loss is not definitely stated; but the following expressions are used, as "very considerable," "profuse," "a gush," "really frightful," "not alarming," "great and welled up." These statements are so vague as to be completely valueless, and cannot enable us to judge whether the patients were really endangered by it. We know too well what varying accounts are given by different persons as to the quantity of blood lost on ordinary occasions, to receive the above terms as evidence of a positively serious loss. It is very probable that the amount of blood lost in most of these cases did not exceed that which is discharged after ordinary labours.

In four of the cases, chloroform was administered; and in one, etherisation was used before and during the operation.

In twelve cases, the placenta was cut upon; in one of which there were twenty to twenty-four ounces of blood lost; in one, fourteen to sixteen ounces; in one, ten to twelve ounces; in two, a considerable quantity was lost; and in seven or eight, the quantity was very trifling.

In two cases, the epigastric artery was divided; but there was little bleeding, and it was readily stopped.

In seven cases, the blood issued from the uterine tissue during the incision.

It has been asserted that these accidents (in Cæsarean cases) depend on causes which are not very much within obstetric control. This statement is, however, very far from true. In the majority, the sources whence the blood flows are, as has already been mentioned, the same as those whence it issues in other cases of flooding.

The complete contraction of the uterus must, if possible, be obtained; and the placenta must be promptly removed. The latter part of this rule can always be easily and effectually carried out; but there is more difficulty to fulfil the former part of it, as the contractility of the organ is considerably impaired. This is a common effect after protracted labour. In most of the Cæsarean cases, the operation was not performed until the power of the uterus was completely worn out; and in many cases its tissue was disorganised. The relative and comparative tolerance of the loss of blood in such cases should be duly considered; and as far as possible this accident should be guarded against. It is not, however, true that "the resources of art can effect but little," or to look upon it as a certain contingency upon the operation.

The vital powers of most of those women who underwent the Cæsarean section were at a very low ebb previously to the commencement of labour, and were further seriously exhausted by its duration.

Inflammation of the peritoneum is considered as a frequent cause of death after the Cæsarean section. This serous membrane is usually more susceptible to morbid disturbance after labour than it is at ordinary times; so that it cannot be wondered at, that this disease is sometimes found in Cæsarean cases, especially if the previous management of the labours, and the real condition of the patients at the time of the operation, are duly considered. The duration of the labours of the women who had peritonitis is as follows.

In one, it was six days; in one, three days; in one, sixty-one hours; in one, sixty hours; in one, fifty-three hours; in one, fifty-two hours; in one, forty-eight hours; in one, forty hours; in one, thirty-eight hours (craniotomy was unsuccessfully performed in this case); in one, thirty hours (turning was unsuccessfully attempted, and craniotomy was afterwards ineffectually performed); in one, eighty-two hours (attempts were unsuccessfully made, the membranes being ruptured, to induce premature labour; and afterwards craniotomy was performed without success). Other periods are to be noted—twenty-four, twenty-nine hours, etc.; and in one the labour lasted only thirteen hours, but in this case the uterus was stitched with the glover's suture. In one woman, the duration of her labour was fifty-four hours; she had flooding before the operation. In another woman, whose labour lasted ten days, it is stated that she had peritoneal inflammation, in conjunction with the effect of shock.

In two or three cases, the lower portion of the cervix and the os uteri were gangrenous. The violent and constant pressure of these portions of the uterus betwixt the head of the infant and the irregular projection of the distorted pelvis cannot be unlimitedly continued without producing either laceration or disorganisation, or complete destruction, of their tissue.

It is alleged that the abdominal and uterine wounds have been found in very different states, most of which are said to have shown a feeble reparative power and a perverted action.

When the vital powers are good in cases of an operation, we have conservative and restorative action immediately set up; but, if they are impaired by the existence of positive disease, or by protracted labour, unhealthy action takes place; and, instead of healthy surfaces, flabby and œdematous edges of the wound are seen; and, instead of an adhesive effusion, there is a dirty sanious discharge, and the uterine wound is said to be found generally gaping. Although remarks on the bad state of the wounds are made to depreciate the value of the Cæsarean section, yet it cannot be a matter of surprise that they should sometimes present such very unhealthy aspects, if the previous constitutional and local condition of nearly all the women upon whom it has been performed be justly considered.

Another cause of danger is supposed to be the reduction which goes on in the puerperal uterus, so as to regain its pristine size. This change is considered antagonistic to the reparative action necessary to heal the wound made in the Cæsarean section.

The entire vascular system of the puerperal uterus is very considerably altered; and the supply of blood to it is consequently very much lessened from that which existed during its gravid state. This change, together with a process of absorption which is now set up, at least partly causes its diminution of size. But this organ may be, as it is stated, reduced in bulk by a general degradation of its tissue; of which the abundant presence of fat-globules in the lochial discharge, and in the *débris* which covers the interior of the organ, is ample evidence. These are natural changes, and not pathological; and, if there be a reduction of bulk in the uterus, there is simultaneously a relative diminution in the size of the wound. It has yet to be proved whether the alteration which the puerperal uterus naturally undergoes will in any way interfere with the process of reparation.

The want of union of the edges of the uterine wound by adhesion or by granulation is traceable to causes which have already been frequently mentioned, rather than to the natural organic changes above stated.

Tetanus has been considered a cause of maternal death after the Cæsarean operation; but I am not aware that this disease is so recorded in any of the tabulated cases. Professor Dubois told me that a patient of his had an attack of this disease in two or three weeks after the operation, and it proved fatal. This disease, it is said, occurs after other obstetric operations; and it sometimes occurs after abortion.

The bursting open of the wound becomes a cause of danger, by allowing the protrusion of the intestines. The attenuated state of the abdominal parietes, which sometimes exists in extreme cases of mollities ossium, occasions this accident. It happened in three cases, in which no attempts were made either to replace the protruded bowels, or to approximate the retracted integuments. This, however, was a great omission. As an example of the necessity and propriety of returning the intestines, if they unfortunately escape through the wound, I refer to the case (one of recovery) of Mrs. Sankey. (See Appendix.)

Frequent examinations *per vaginam* are often productive of very serious mischief. Inflammation, followed by suppuration and sloughing, are not unusual results. Two or three examples will be found reported, in which great tumefaction of the external genitals and an inflamed state of the vagina existed. These results are alone attributable to frequent and unwarrantable interference.

Long and ineffectual attempts to deliver by the perforator and crotchet are highly dangerous. Contusion, lacerations, inflammation, infiltration, suppuration, and sloughing, are consequences which are not unusually to be found in cases in which violent efforts have been made to drag a mangled infant through a contracted pelvis.

II.—*On the Causes of Infantile Mortality.* The fœtus *in utero* sometimes dies from diseases which occur in its own system, and also from morbid changes in the structure of the placenta, which interrupts the supply of blood from this organ. These causes are not, however, confined in their operation to any particular class of cases. The duration of labour exercises very great influence upon the infant. If the membranes remain entire, and the liquor amnii undischarged, it will endure the continuance and violence of the labour-pains for a considerable length of time without injury. But after this event has happened, there is much more risk of mischief ; and the danger increases in a ratio proportioned to the length of time the labour is protracted. The deaths of the infants which have occurred in Cæsarean cases are generally to be attributed to the long continued and violent pressure which they have endured during labour.

There is, however, another cause of infantile death which more especially belongs to the Cæsarean section. I mean the spasmodic seizure of the neck or body of the infant during its extraction through the incised opening of the uterus. In general, there is no difficulty experienced in these cases in withdrawing the infant from the uterus ; but sometimes some portion of its body becomes so firmly grasped by the uterus in its passage through the incised opening that great difficulty is experienced in extracting it. There is, however, more danger to the infant when the neck is seized by the uterine grasp than when it is held by any other part of its body. In such cases the body of the infant has been most easily brought along until the shoulder had passed, when the neck is instantaneously seized, and so firmly held, as to require long and continued efforts to be made in order to extricate the head.

The fact, that the uterus in natural labour is energetically roused to expel the placenta which has been separated, first led me to attribute the seizure of the neck of the child during the Cæsarean section to the partial or complete detachment of the placenta. It has lately been doubted whether this theory will suffice to explain it, as "numerous instances are recorded in which the placenta either protruded through the incision, or was found lying loose in the uterine cavity, and in which no inordinate contraction ensued." I am, and was from the first, aware of the truth of this assertion, from an accurate analysis and tabulation of all the published cases; but, notwithstanding the apparent force of this objection, my opinion remains the same.

There are seven cases (two within my own knowledge) in which this event happened; and, as far as I can ascertain, the placenta has been partially or entirely detached in all these cases, or at least presumptively so.

How far the violent uterine action may resemble the spasm of hour-glass contraction, I cannot determine; yet analogy would lead me to think it did.

There is only recorded one (another case) in which the infant was grasped round the abdomen above the hips; the head, shoulders, and trunk, having been first drawn forth. The child was previously dead; and the only effect recognised was the squeezing out the meconium into the uterine cavity. Turning had been unsuccessfully attempted; and during this operation, it was found that there was hour-glass contraction. Does not the occurrence of hour-glass contraction before, and seizure of the child's hips after, the operation, favour the above mentioned opinion?

CHAPTER IV.

On the Performance of the Cæsarean Section, etc.

THE process adopted by Nature in some of those cases of labour in which she cannot overcome the obstacle which prevents the passage of the infant through the pelvis, is, in the first instance, the yielding of the uterine tissue, thereby making an opening for its escape. Afterwards, if the constitutional powers prove equal to the entire process, an incasement of the fœtus is effected by the effusion of lymph. And, after a time, a pointing in some part of the abdominal parietes shows itself, which is soon followed by ulceration, and part after part of the infant passes through the opening, until the whole contents of the cyst are discharged. This is a very slow and hazardous process.

In adopting the Cæsarean section, we in some measure imitate Nature in her attempt to remove the infant, although by a much more safe and an expeditious plan.

This operation ought not to be made one of display. There should only be a very few persons present; and the greatest quietude should be afforded to the patient. Every cause likely in any way to create unpleasant emotional feeling should be most carefully avoided. These rules were strictly observed in the two successful cases in which I was engaged. It is of the first importance, when possible, to adopt all such measures as will prepare the patient to undergo this operation, by improving the general health.

The bowels should be emptied by a large quantity of warm water thrown into the rectum and colon, by an enema-apparatus with a long flexible tube (like the one used to enter the stomach), so that its extremity can reach beyond the great projection of the sacrum.

The bladder must also be emptied by a catheter, equal in length to that used for the male. This organ is forced downwards and forwards, and lies under the deflected uterus, whereby its cervix is lengthened and compressed upon the pubes. This altered position of the bladder is particularly to be observed during the latter month of pregnancy, in cases of pelvic distortion from mollities ossium. Frequent examinations *per vaginam* have been already shown to be extremely injurious; so that this practice should not be allowed. In an exploration made to ascertain the measurement of a distorted pelvis, the obstetrician is compelled to pass his hand completely, and as far as possible, into the vagina. Anxious to ascertain the state of the os uteri, the presentation of the infant, and the exact available space in the pelvis, he prolongs the operation, and often repeats it. And when consultations are numerous (as is too common) in these cases, serious mischief is inflicted on the pelvic organs and tissue. By one effectual examination, every necessary information may be obtained. The interest of the patient is best secured by having only a limited number (say two persons) in consultation.

The operation should be performed on the bed; so that the patient may be kept as quiet as possible afterwards. In some of the cases in which the woman was removed to a table, some untoward circumstance happened.

The temperature of the room should be regulated, and a genial warmth of the atmosphere maintained.

The uterus projects more or less forwards; and when the pelvic distortion is caused by mollities ossium, this organ assumes the retort shape. Its projection is so great, that its normal anterior surface rests upon the thighs of the patient when she sits, so that the fundus necessarily stands most foremost. Before the incision is made, it is of the utmost consequence to raise the deflected uterus up; or else the fundal tissue, which abounds with large anastomosing vessels, must unavoidably be divided. Neglect of this caution has, no doubt, led to the hæmorrhage which happened in some of the cases. A division of the structure of the upper part of the fundus of the uterus must certainly interfere with the regular or efficient contraction of this organ, and thereby produce a gaping character of the wound.

When we contemplate the mischievous effects of protracted labour, and review the unfavourable condition in which most of the patients have been brought by unwisely procrastinating the operation, we must at once be convinced how important it is to perform it early. The sooner the better it is had recourse to after it is determined upon, either as one of election or one of necessity.

When labour is rendered difficult by great distortion of the pelvis, or by large exostoses, or by large tumours in its cavity, some of those natural organic changes are not to be found, which would otherwise guide us, and enable us to judge of its commencement and progress. To wait, then, in such cases as these for the dilatation of the os uteri is not only a great mistake, but also a very great evil; for, in most of them, this part of the uterus cannot be touched, and, in general, very little dilatation of it does or can take place.

The dangers of delay, on expectant grounds like these, which so frequently happened in the registered cases, ought to guard us against waiting for those indications which cannot possibly be discovered, and induce us to operate early. As soon as the labour is established, and before or immediately after the membranes are ruptured, is the most favourable time 'to proceed. Great advantage accrues from adopting this plan; for the length of the uterine incision would relatively diminish in size, equal to the diminution which takes place by the contraction of the uterus. Another great advantage arising from this course is, that the danger of protraction would altogether be avoided. It is a well known fact, that little risk comparatively occurs before the waters are discharged.

Before the incision is made, the location of the placenta should, if possible, be ascertained, in order to avoid its being wounded. In the 77 cases, it is reported as follows. In 29 it was connected to the fore part of the uterus; of this number, in 2 it was placed towards the fundus; in 13 it was cut upon. In 10 cases, it was adherent on or towards the back part of the uterus. In 31 cases, the position of it is not alluded to; and, therefore, it is to be presumed it was posteriorly placed. In 5 cases, it occupied the fundus; in 1 case, it was found near the left Fallopian tube; and in one case, it was attached (placenta prævia) over the os uteri.

This minute inquiry as to the precise fixture of the placenta has not been made merely for the purpose of suggesting rules of caution which ought to be observed before making the incision; but, also, of proving that this organ has not a definite position assigned to it.

It is, then, of the greatest importance to make the incision so as to avoid, if possible, cutting upon the placenta; as considerable danger may accrue from so doing.

The stethoscope will nearly always enable us to avoid these hazards. By it we derive positive information of the infant's life, by hearing distinctly the pulsations of its heart; and it affords us negative evidence of the infant's death, when no cardiac sounds are perceived through it. The audibility of the "placental *soufflet*" directs us to investigate the quarter from whence the murmurs proceed; and by attention, we may nearly always assure ourselves in what vicinity of the uterus the placenta is fixed. If this sound is not heard, we have a right to conclude that this organ is not within the reach of the knife if the infant be still alive. If it be dead, no great risk will be incurred if the placenta be divided, as the vascular function of this organ will then, doubtless, have ceased.

The position and direction of the external incision has varied. In 57 cases, it has been made longitudinally; in 11 of which number, it was made on the right side; in 24 cases, it was made on the left side; and in 22 cases, it was made in the centre of the abdomen. In 2 cases, it had a transverse direction on the right side. In one, it was made obliquely on the right side. In 17 cases, the situation and direction of the wound is not recorded.

I prefer the wound to be longitudinal, and on the left side.

There are no tissues concerned in the operation which require very slow or nice dissection; therefore, unnecessary tediousness should be especially avoided. If the uterus be slowly incised, the stimulus of the knife instantaneously throws this organ in violent and irregular contraction, which separates the placenta, and entails mischief on both the mother and the infant. Every precaution having been taken, we ought to strictly observe the motto, "*Cito et tuto*". The incision should be made on the body of the uterus, because this portion of the organ is eminently contractile, and ought to extend well towards the fundus, but not into it. It ought not, however, to be carried too far down into the cervix uteri, because this part possesses dilatable properties which are unfavourable to a diminution in the size of the wound.

When the uterine incision is completed, there should be no delay in withdrawing the infant. When it lays in its usual natural position, with the head over the brim of the pelvis, then the obstetrician should seize its legs with his right hand, and pass his left cautiously and quickly down so as to embrace the face on one side, or the hind part of its head. By this mode, a double power could be effectually exerted: one of traction by the legs, the other by raising the head upwards.

If the breech offer at the incised uterine opening, the practitioner should seize it with his right hand and withdraw it, and at the same time use his left hand as above mentioned. If the head lay in proximity with the incision, then it ought first to be brought forth, and, at the same time, he should pass one hand cautiously forward along its body so as fairly to embrace the breech, and act with both his hands as recommended above. These precautionary rules are suggested to prevent the grasping seizure of the neck or the hips of the infant, as the case may be, during its removal. (*Vide* remarks already made.) One or two writers have urged, that the head of the infant should be always first extracted, on the grounds of being safer for it; but a conditional practice, according to its position in the uterus, is by far the best.

The head is most generally situated in the lower segment of the womb, and, therefore, at some distance from the centre of the incision. In order to bring it fairly to the opening, it would produce a great strain on, if not laceration of, the contracted uterine tissue, and create nearly a doubling of the child upon itself before it could be extracted. And as expedition is required, it would be found that the bulk of the head was not very readily grasped with sufficient firmness so as to ensure its speedy withdrawal. Time would be lost, and impediments added. The placenta, with the membranes, should be also quickly extracted.

Protrusion of the intestines is very apt to occur during the operation; this becomes very troublesome to the operator and distressing to the patient, and a considerable time is consumed in order to replace them. This accident not only predisposes to remote mischief; but it immediately tends to depress the vital powers of the woman. She feels faint, and has a sense of sinking. Every care should, therefore, be taken by the assistants to repress and retain these viscera under the integuments by an extended application of both hands on each side of the incision. It is of the utmost importance, that the edges of the external wound should be effectually secured. Sutures or pins ought to be inserted at very short distances; and a considerable extent of the parietes (not embracing the peritoneum) should be included, especially in those cases in which the integuments are much attenuated.

The after-management of the patient must be conducted on recognised medical and surgical principles. Much mischief has been done by active treatment; and it should never be forgotten that, even if it be thought desirable to pursue this plan, it should always be relative to the state of the woman. A negative treatment has been found by me most advantageous. Opium, in full doses if required, should be given.

It is now a general practice to administer chloroform before and during the performance of important operations. If cautiously used, the data already accumulated justify the inference that it is of great advantage to the surgeon, by inducing a state of resistless quietude of the patient. The severity of the pain inflicted by the knife is considerably lessened, and the shock to the nervous system is thereby diminished. In the majority of surgical operations, there are no other contingent circumstances relative to the administration of this drug which require the attention of the operator, except the necessity of his having first ascertained whether there exist any organic disease of the heart or large vessels which would be dangerously influenced by it; but it is otherwise when it is proposed to use it in a Cæsarean case.

The incision made into the uterus must be at first necessarily large, to enable the obstetrician to extract the infant and the placenta; but, after their removal, the length of the wound is very considerably diminished by the contraction of this organ, which, if not interrupted, is both instantaneous and energetic, thereby effectually preventing any great loss of blood. It is, therefore, very important to inquire whether chloroform interferes with, or altogether suspends, this normal contraction; or whether it induces this action *de novo*, or strengthens it in intensity.

Chloroform has been inhaled in fifteen Cæsarean cases: in one of which there was hæmorrhage; in two of which there was very little blood lost; one of which cases, it is stated, was benefited by its inhalation; and in three instances the discharge of blood was considerable, two of which proved fatal. One of these cases, however, recovered. In one of the cases, the uterus did not contract much; in one, the hand was pressed upon it to induce contraction; in four cases, it is stated, that this organ contracted well. Three of these patients were completely unconscious; and one (which I saw) was only partially under the influence of chloroform.

Ether was administered in one case in which there was some bleeding, but not so much as to be considered to be alarming.

Obstetricians differ in opinion as to the positive effects of chloroform on the uterus. Some say uterine action is retarded by it. Others, again, assert that it does not interfere with it; and there are others who affirm that it promotes and strengthens it. The data which exist on this subject are very meagre and very contradictory ; and, therefore, with such discrepancy of opinion, it is impossible to come to a satisfactory conclusion on this subject, especially in reference to its use in Cæsarean cases, in which it is of the highest importance that the normal action of the uterus should not be disturbed. It would, however, be most advantageous to the patient, if she could be safely spared the pain inflicted by the operation ; although not one of those women in whose cases I was concerned complained of pain during its performance, but, on the contrary, bore it with great moral courage and fortitude ; and most of them observed that they suffered less from the incision, than the anguish they had endured from one of the unavailing labour-pains.

The disturbed state of the vascular and nervous system in all those women who have undergone this operation, must most assuredly render them unfit subjects for chloroform ; and, therefore, the deductions which may be drawn from the results in these cases in which the women laboured under incurable disease, and were exhausted from protracted labour, ought not to prejudice us altogether against its use.

We find that vomiting occurred in eleven of the sixteen cases in which chloroform had been administered. In two of the cases, the abdominal wound was rent open by the violent efforts induced ; and in several of the others, disagreeable effects ensued. If chloroform do really produce vomiting and its injurious effects, there can be no doubt it ought to be discarded, as it is most important to keep the patient free from all causes which have a tendency to disturb the reparative process in the wound.

So long as the Cæsarean operation is considered only one of necessity, and its performance so unwisely and so cruelly delayed, great risk must attend the inhalation of chloroform. But, if it be made an operation of election, so that women who are in a better constitutional state undergo it, and if, likewise, it be timely performed, then it may be found that great advantage may be derived from the use of this drug ; but, nevertheless, before we acknowledge chloroform as a recognised means for this operation, we ought to be fully satisfied what effects it produces on the uterus.

CHAPTER V.

Other Obstetric Operations.

THE other obstetric operations which require to be now considered
are reduced into two classes, one of which includes those measures
which are to be adopted compatibly with the preservation of the
lives of both the mother and the infant. This division embraces
the Employment of the Long Forceps, Turning, and the Induction
of Premature Labour. The other class of obstetric operations are
those by which the life of the infant, or that of the embryo, as the
case may respectively be, must be sacrificed; namely, Craniotomy,
Embryotomy, and the Induction of Abortion.

I shall make a few remarks on a suggested plan for Dilating the
Distorted Pelvis; and I shall also briefly mention Symphyseotomy.

The objects to be attained by these two classes of operations are
very differently estimated by different obstetricians. Some consider
that those measures by which the lives of both mother and child
are preserved, are adopted solely for the purpose of lessening the too
frequent employment of craniotomy; others consider them as appli-
cable to prevent the performance of the Cæsarean section. But few
practitioners would ever think of having recourse to this latter
named operation in cases in which either the long forceps, turning,
or the induction of premature labour, could be successfully employed.
The latter class of operations are performed with the express object
and intention, as far as possible, to supersede the Cæsarean section.

CHAPTER VI.

Operations intended to save the Life of the Mother, and also that of the Infant.

I.—*On the Employment of the Long Forceps.* This instrument most justly takes a high position in obstetricy, because its sole employment is for the preservation of life. It is intended, within a certain range of protracted labour, to supersede craniotomy. In the hands of a discreet and judicious practitioner, it is both a safe and a very powerful instrument. Before its introduction into practice, whenever turning could not be performed, the child was doomed to destruction by craniotomy. The employment of the long forceps in this country has been very tardily recognised. When I commenced (1817) my professional career, this instrument had never been used in Manchester; but, having heard the valuable remarks of Dr. Haighton upon its use, I availed myself of the first opportunity of making trial of it. I employed his instrument; but, after repeated trials, I abandoned it, and contrived one of my own, with blades of equal length, but with parallel shanks. This instrument I also found tended, in its embrace and compression of the infant's head, to produce disagreeable effects upon it, which I endeavoured by a second contrivance to obviate. This instrument is so constructed that only a limited degree of compression can be exercised. It has very short handles, and consists of blades of an unequal length: one, the long one, to lie over the face; the other, the short one, to be placed over the occiput. By this arrangement, the head of the infant is placed in the most favourable position within their grasp, and none of the injuries are inflicted upon it which are found when forceps with equal blades and long compressing handles are used. This instrument is employed mainly as a tractor, and very limitedly as a compressor.

To save the life of the child by the use of the long forceps is, doubtless, the object of every obstetrician ; for, unless this were his intention, it would be better at once to have recourse to craniotomy. The head of the child cannot bear more than a certain degree of pressure compatible with its life ; and, although it is wisely ordained that it can safely bear a greater degree of pressure before than after birth, yet there is a limit even here, beyond which it cannot be carried without the destruction of the infant's life. The head can also bear a greater degree of pressure when the force is applied in one direction, than it can in another. Much greater compressing force can be more safely used when exercised in the bi-parietal, than when applied in the occipito-frontal diameter. As the long forceps are usually placed on the head of the infant so as to embrace it in its long diameter, we ought therefore to consider whether our instrument is so constructed as to permit such an undue degree of pressure as may prove unfavourable to the life of the infant.

The head of the infant, when it is situated at the brim of the pelvis, usually lies with its fronto-occipital diameter corresponding to one of the oblique diameters of the pelvis ; the vertex or face being placed towards the right or towards the left acetabulum. But when the antero-posterior diameter of the pelvis is shortened by the sacrum projecting more forwards, the head assumes a more directly transverse position. Now, in this position of the head, it is most desirable to place the two blades of the forceps on the sides of the pelvis, so that one blade lies over the face, and the other over the occiput of the infant. In this case, the instrument embraces the head in the most unfavourable direction for its safety, if forcible compression be made. But the lateral pelvic position of the blades of this instrument is much safer for the maternal pelvic organs than if, as recommended by some practitioners, they were placed in the conjugate diameter. To add the bulk of the instrument to the already diminished capacity of this part of the pelvis would be unwise. In all our artificial appliances, we ought to endeavour to produce similar changes on the head of the infant, which nature accomplishes, if left unaided. The head is lengthened, and its rounded shape changed ; whilst its bi-parietal diameter is lessened. The former change we ought to obtain by having the instrument so formed as to allow the head to elongate when traction is used, and by the pressure it receives from the anterior and posterior parts of the pelvis. Notwithstanding the high opinions expressed of the great advantages of compression, I am convinced it is mischievous. This statement is not theoretical, but rests on facts derived from the use of the long forceps both as a strong compressor, and, as now recommended, a tractor with very slight compressing power. In truth, I cannot understand how effective compression can be made, unless the blades of the forceps are applied on the sides of the head, and on the anterior and posterior parts of the pelvis. The tractive power of my instrument is increased by having a handkerchief passed through an opening in the shanks, which is formed by nearly a semicircular curve in each shank near the handles. The handles should be only slightly tied, to maintain their position. A pendulum, or side-to-side movement, must be combined with the traction; taking care that the range is regulated by the line of the axis of the pelvis, and that no pressure be thrown upon the maternal pelvic structures.

This instrument is sometimes required to rectify the position of the head of the infant, when its long diameter lies parallel with the antero-posterior diameter of the pelvis; the face lying either towards the pubes or towards the sacrum. In such cases, the blades of the forceps should be introduced along the sides of the pelvis, but should be placed over the parietal bones of the head. (For a further exposition upon these questions, I refer my reader to essays on various subjects connected with midwifery.)

There are no statistics published which afford any truthful information either as to the frequency of the application of this instrument, or as to the mortality of those women who have been delivered by it. In my own practice, I have used this instrument very frequently; and I can most conscientiously assert that I never had a death as a result of its application. In cases in which craniotomy had been performed, in some once, in others several times, under the management of different practitioners, I have delivered the women by this instrument, and saved the children. It is the duty of the obstetrician to keep constantly before his mind the dangers of protraction, and recollect that these increase in a ratio (already stated) proportioned to the length of time the labour is prolonged.

If this instrument is to fully accomplish its capabilities of saving life, it must be used before those dreadful mischiefs are produced by delay. If we calculate to bring a head through a fixed pelvic space, we ought to remember that this space is considerably lessened by the effects of long continued pressure.

The dogmatic injunctions of present and former authors, that the forceps ought not to be used before the os uteri is fully dilated, or until the woman has been in labour a certain number of hours, or until the ear of the child can be felt, are highly dangerous. They are delusive, and would, if acted upon, altogether prevent the use of the long forceps.

If these alleged conditions are required to exist to guide the practitioner when he ought to have recourse to this instrument, these rules are tantamount to a complete interdiction of its use. In fact, they are too absurd, unfounded, and dangerous, as indications of the propriety of even using the short forceps.

To wait for the dilatation of the os uteri after the rupture of the membranes is a great mistake; for, in the great majority of cases which require aid by the long forceps, this organic change cannot take place. The obstacle being at the brim of the pelvis, the head of the infant cannot be pressed down upon it; so that, before this change happens, irretrievable mischief may be inflicted by the continued pressure which the pelvic tissues must, under such circumstances, endure. Therefore, as soon as the time has arrived for delivery, we must not hesitate to apply the long forceps, provided the os uteri is so far dilated, and further dilatable, to enable the practitioner safely to introduce the blades.

If the instrument is in the hands of a discreet and judicious obstetrician, no mischief need be dreaded; for the blades of a well-made instrument will rest as safely within the uterus as the hand of the practitioner.

Time ought never to be considered an element of calculation, especially during the second stage of labour, for the use of instruments, except in creating an anxiety to be on the watch, and to take timely steps to deliver the patient.

An early use of the long forceps, when the necessity of the case is established, will prevent those serious constitutional and local mischiefs (already mentioned) which are produced by the long continued pressure of the head of the infant upon the pelvic organs and tissues. Those who are opposed to the use of instruments, and advocate time and patience, attribute to their application those structural and organic lesions which are really the effects of delay.

It has been already stated, that the head of the infant can only safely bear a certain amount of compression by the forceps; but it must also be understood, that the infant is frequently destroyed by injury inflicted upon the head during protracted labour. Procrastination beyond a certain limit is highly hazardous to its life; and, as its preservation is an important object to attain, the long forceps should be immediately applied (if safe to the mother), if the stethoscope indicates danger.

In convulsions occurring during labour, these instruments may be of essential benefit, if they can be safely used.

In cases of accidental, and also in some cases of partial, attachment of the placenta over the os uteri, this instrument has great advantages over other means, if the os uteri is dilated and dilatable, when the vital powers are very considerably depressed.

In some cases of rupture of the uterus, in which the child does not recede, and if there is sufficient pelvic space, and if all other requisite changes exist for their safe introduction, then there may be a remote chance of saving the infant's life by their use.

In cases of arrest from exhaustion, and even in fatal syncope, this instrument may be usefully employed. In some cases of face-presentations, and other unfavourable positions of the head, the application of the long forceps will be found most advantageous. The want of relative proportion between the infant's head, being abnormally large, or too firmly ossified to allow a necessary diminution in its size, in order to pass into and through the pelvis, are causes of protracted labour; and, when the obstacles are so great as to oppose the head passing through the brim of the pelvis, the long forceps will be required to effect the delivery. When the pelvis is relatively too small in its general conformation, from premature defect of development, or when it partakes too much of the male conformation, or in the slight oblique-shaped pelvis of Naegele, or when the pelvic bones have been fractured and there has been irregular union (I have a cast of a pelvis which had been fractured, and which in character now resembles the oblique of Naegele), or when small sized exostoses or loose or fixed tumours occupy the pelvis, the long forceps may be requisite and effectual in the delivery; but, in all these cases, the practice must be determined by the available space which exists in each case.

Those cases in which the value and powers of this instrument are most conspicuous are those in which the brim of the pelvis is diminished in its antero-posterior diameter, either by rickets or by mollities ossium.

In the slighter pelvic deformities produced by rickets, the brim is often considerably lessened in its conjugate diameter, whilst the cavity and outlet are not very much altered either in size or in shape; so that the obstacle to the descent of the head is chiefly confined to the brim. But, in a pelvis distorted by mollities ossium, the diminution in its capacity is not confined to any one portion, but the brim, cavity, and outlet suffer in a greater or less degree; so that, when delivery by the long forceps is contemplated, the character of the distortion must be well considered.

It must be obvious to every well informed obstetrician, that the head of the infant can be more easily brought through a pelvis distorted by rickets, than through one distorted by mollities ossium; assuming that the antero-posterior measurements are the same in both. Opinions as to the space required to bring the head through the pelvis by the long forceps differ very considerably; and, on reflection, this variation is not to be wondered at. It is at all times difficult to arrive at an arithmetical accuracy by a vaginal examination of the different character of distortion just alluded to. The difference in the size of heads of infants, and likewise the different degrees of ossification, must all tend to influence the result. But, notwithstanding these uncertainties, it is desirable that I should state my opinion as to the smallest space at the brim of the pelvis through which the obstetrician would be warranted in attempting to extract the infant by means of the long forceps. Knowing as I do the great responsibility I incur in making positive assertions on practical points of such importance, yet, as I have by trial proved the truth of my statement, I hope I shall not be charged with temerity. I have the more confidence in giving my opinion on this point, because it is certain that, if this instrument cannot be successfully used, the life of the infant would have to be sacrificed. I would, therefore, rather run the risk of committing a venial error by leaning to the side of mercy, by recommending, in the first place, a cautious trial of the long forceps where there was the least doubt in the mind of the practitioner as to the precise pelvic measurement, and thereby give the benefit of the doubt to the unborn babe. With this feeling, I then say that, where the distance from sacrum to pubes is three inches, and a fraction under, and there exists sufficient space in the transverse diameter, an experienced practitioner ought to make a cautious and persevering trial of the long forceps before he has recourse to craniotomy. This opinion is advisedly given, because it is quite impossible to compute either the positive and relative space of the pelvis, or the size, compressibility, or other conditions of the head of the infant, with such mathematical certainty as to warrant any person to destroy life.

II.—*On Turning in Cases of Slight Distortion of the Pelvis.* Turning, in cases of slight distortion of the pelvis, justly ranks as a conservative operation. Turning was formerly had recourse to in all difficult labours in which craniotomy was not performed, because the use of the forceps was not known at that time ; but, after Chamberleyn's discovery, this practice gradually sank in the estimation of obstetricians.

The thanks of the profession are due to Professor Simpson for the revival of this operation, and for the clear and lucid manner in which he has enforced his opinions both by argument and statistical data. He advocates turning in cases of slight distortion of the pelvis, and considers that the base of the head of an infant will pass with more facility and through a smaller aperture, when brought first, as in footling cases, than when it passes last, as in ordinary head-presentations. This doctrine, however, I ventured to differ from (see *Provincial Medical and Surgical Journal*, vol. ii, p. 3) ; and it has been more recently doubted by Dr. McClintock (*Obstetrical Transactions*, vol. iv, p. 175). At that time, I considered perforation, if required after turning had been performed, would be more difficult and more hazardous. This opinion has been also lately expressed by Dr. McClintock.

Notwithstanding my former opinion, above referred to, and the opinion I now hold, that turning in cases of protracted labour, from the slighter contractions at the brim of the pelvis, cannot ever become an alternative operation for the use of the long forceps. There are, doubtlesss some cases in which turning would deserve a preference ; and, in the hands of some practitioners, it might be more safely undertaken.

The merit of the professor, in trying to establish this as an alternative operation, is in the intention to abolish, as far as possible, craniotomy.

" This practice of turning, in cases of pelvic deformity, is one of the agitated questions of the present day, which requires the sober and dispassionate consideration of all who are interested in the establishment and advance of obstetrics."

This question can only be settled by a long accumulation of practical facts and comparative trials. Mere opinion can make no approach towards its settlement.

F

The danger of turning will be considerably diminished when the plan of internal and external version, as recommended by Dr. Hicks, is adopted. (Vide *Obstet. Trans.*, vol. v, p. 219 ; also his essay.)

In the performance of turning, I prefer and recommend the operator to seize one foot or one knee, for reasons set forth in my essays on various midwifery subjects. The funis is thereby better defended, and the egress of the head is rendered safer and easier by a partial breech-case having preceded it.

Dr. McClintock, "after having seized one leg and brought it into the vagina, could not, with all the force he could use, make the child revolve." He quotes the opinion of Madame La Chapelle, who speaks of the difficulty of effecting version by one leg when the head presents. She says the difficulty is produced by the head being pushed into the brim before the breech. It is quite evident that the cause which opposed the revolution of the child was, not taking hold and bringing down one leg, but the result of protracted labour after the rupture of the membranes. The head was forcibly pushed down upon or partially into the pelvis ; and the uterus was doubtless violently, and perhaps spasmodically, contracted upon the infant's body, moulding and applying itself to all its hollows and projections.

As turning, in the cases of slighter distortion of the pelvis, is intended to save the child, this operation ought to be early performed—before, or as soon as possible after, the discharge of the liquor amnii. In cases which have been unduly procrastinated after this event has happened, and when the uterus is strongly embracing the infant, violent attempts to turn ought not to be made until some plan has been adopted to lessen the irritability of the uterus, and relax as far as possible its tonic and alternate contraction. Venesection and opiates are appropriate remedies. Does chloroform relax the uterus?

The death of the infant after the operation of turning (if it be living when this operation is commenced) is most frequently caused by the practitioner hurrying too rapidly its delivery after the revolution has been made. Time should be first given for the uterus to adjust itself to the changed position of the infant. When extractive force is used, it should at first be slow and gentle, and, if possible, in cooperation with uterine contraction. If the infant be rapidly and forcibly dragged through the pelvis, the chin leaves the breast, and is tilted upwards, thereby creating an unfavourable relative position between the diameters of the head and those of the pelvis. A great difficulty is now found to exist, which opposes an easy entrance of the head into the brim. Another mischief happens from attempts to draw the infant too quickly along by bringing the too bulky part of the infant (the head) to press upon and distend the os and cervix uteri before these parts are prepared to bear the change ; and, consequently, spasmodic retention takes place, which is often so violent and obstinate as to cause the death of the infant.

III.—*On Premature Labour.* The induction of premature labour was first performed by Dr. Macaulay in England in the year 1756. But, although this is the fact, and though the importance of the operation is acknowledged and its adoption sanctioned by the most eminent British obstetricians, yet, if we consult statistics, we shall find it has only been limitedly employed, in comparison with its practical importance. There is no recognition of this practice in the statute-book, to distinguish it from that abuse of it which is committed for criminal purposes. In this respect, it is estimated in the same way as some other operations which I shall consider in the subsequent part of these remarks, being only sanctioned by the law of custom. This is an unwise legislative omission, because it permits wicked men to cover their crimes under the pretension of a legitimate act. On this account, therefore, great caution should be exercised whenever this operation is intended to be performed. It is justifiable on moral grounds, and it is approved of on every professional and social principle. The object of its performance is noble and humane, as the lives of those infants are saved by it which must otherwise be destroyed ; whilst at the same time, according to my experience, the woman incurs little risk, if any more than that which is contingent on ordinary labour, and very much less than that which results from craniotomy. But, notwithstanding its high value, it ought never to be performed without great necessity, nor without having been first well considered and sanctioned by a consultation.

It is a simple, safe, and efficacious operation, and, if duly performed, infants not to be computed in number would be born alive ; it saves when its alternative assuredly destroys. It is not intended to supersede the Cæsarean section, for no right-minded practitioner would ever think of adopting such a course if the operation now under consideration were eligible ; but the great object to keep in view is, to prevent as far as possible the performance of craniotomy. It has, however, been asserted by one writer, " that premature labour should never be attempted before it has been proved, by the event of one or more destructive fœtal births, that the pelvis was so much distorted that life must have been unavoidably sacrificed before delivery could be accomplished, because a single fatal instance is not always a sufficient warrant for the operation."

The destruction of one infant ought to satisfy every obstetrician that premature labour in a future pregnancy ought to be induced, if the pelvis is so contracted that one full grown cannot possibly pass through it. A second life ought never to be sacrificed in such a case. But, in case such a pelvic deformity were suspected, and, after a careful examination, proved to exist, it would be highly improper to allow a woman to go on to the full period of pregnancy, in order to prove by craniotomy the necessity for the induction of premature labour.

The longer gestation is allowed to proceed before the performance of this operation, a greater chance of living is given to the infant; but the precise period at which labour ought to be induced must entirely depend on the degree of positive or relative diminution in the pelvis.

The express object of the obstetrician is to save the infant; and, therefore, he should allow a sufficient length of time for its intrauterine existence, so as to enable it to support an extrauterine life. Most writers assert that it is not viable before the end of the seventh month of pregnancy; but I think it will live after a shorter sojourn in the uterus. Well authenticated cases are recorded of infants having lived who were born at six and at six and a half months. Similar cases have occurred in my own practice, and also in that of some of my British and foreign medical friends.

The following table shows the progressive development of the fœtal head which takes place during pregnancy, from the fifth and half month up to the ninth.

Date of pregnancy.	Bi-parietal diameter.	Occipito-frontal diameter.
At 5½ months	$2\frac{5}{12}$ inches	$3\frac{5}{12}$ inches
At 6 months	$2\frac{7}{12}$ inches	$3\frac{7}{12}$ inches
At 6½ months	$2\frac{8}{12}$ inches	$3\frac{8}{12}$ inches
At 7 months	$2\frac{9}{12}$ inches	$3\frac{1}{2}$ inches
At 7½ months	$2\frac{10}{12}$ inches	$3\frac{6}{12}$ inches
At 8 months	$3\frac{5}{12}$ inches	4 inches
At 9 months	$3\frac{1}{2}$ inches	$4\frac{5}{12}$ inches

The above measurements strikingly show that the size of the head will be found greater or less according to the period of pregnancy at which artificial labour is brought on; and the size of each must be relatively compared with the varying pelvic cavity through which any of them have to pass. The pelvis may be only just so much diminished in size as not to permit the passage of an infant at the seventh month, and yet allow an easy transmission of one at the sixth or even at the sixth and a half month. A very slight addition of bulk to the head, or a very little diminution of space in the pelvis, will mechanically oppose the passage of the infant; and, on the contrary, a very little comparative difference in either case will render its egress easy. This fact is exemplified by a very simple experiment. Add a little gold-beater's skin to a ball turned to the size or of the diameter of the space it would only just pass through, and this slight addition will be found sufficient to resist its passage.

In correspondence, then, with the facts just mentioned, I have ventured to recommend for consideration the induction of labour at the end of the sixth and the end of the sixth and a half months of pregnancy, in those cases in which the pelvic space is below that which is required for the safe delivery of an infant at the end of the seventh month.

The gradual development of the infant's head during pregnancy should never be forgotten when this operation is contemplated; and it is of equal importance accurately to measure the pelvis, in order that a correct relative comparison may be made. But if the calculation has been erroneous, and the head cannot pass unassisted, then, under such circumstances, the long forceps ought to be applied.

The value of the long forceps should not in all such cases be merely estimated as an accidental contingent auxiliary power; but, in some, this instrument from the first should be considered and accepted as an essential means for delivery.

The combination of these two operations will enable the obstetrician to safely extract a living infant which must otherwise be destroyed. This operation stands preeminently forward as conservative; and, as its mission is for the saving of both the lives, perhaps it may be said to be specially intended for the salvation of the infant which must otherwise be destroyed. We ought, in every case of difficult labour, whether terminated by forceps, or by turning, or by craniotomy, strictly and minutely to examine and ascertain the precise measurement of the pelvis, so as to be able to compute the advantages and disadvantages which are contingent on any of these modes of delivery, when compared to those of the induction of premature labour.

My remarks have been more particularly directed to the induction of premature labour in cases in which the pelvis is positively distorted. But it must be understood that, in all cases in which there is such a relative disproportion between the head of a full-grown infant and the available pelvic space, that the head cannot pass without a reduction of the size by craniotomy, while the pelvis is of such capacity as would permit one less (still viable) advanced to pass through at the above specified periods, premature labour ought to be induced; such as when the pelvis is regular in shape and symmetrical, yet too small from want of development; or when an exostosis has grown from some portion of it, or fixed solid tumours exist within it. It is also sometimes desirable to shorten the period of pregnancy in some diseases which threaten the life of the woman, as in some cases of albuminuria, or when violent uncontrollable vomiting exists.

If this operation be undertaken, subject to the restriction inculcated in these remarks, there can be no question as to the morality of the practice in such cases.

A very important object in medical jurisprudence is also gained by the practice of inducing premature labour at these specified periods of pregnancy. According to the English law, the descent of property is in some cases governed by the state of the infant when born. If it be living, or so far alive that the slightest vital movements could be perceived, such as a quivering of the lips, or the twinkling of the eye-lids, then, under such circumstances, the husband would become entitled (by what is termed "the tenant by the courtesy of England") to the property. But if the infant be dead, then the right of inheritance passes in the line of consanguinity. A case illustrative of the above remarks occurred to Dr. Denman. (*Vide* Beck, and Dr. Paris and Fonblanque.)

Before the operation for the induction of premature labour is performed, the obstetrician should have fully acquainted himself with the relative measurements of the head of the infant and the pelvic space through which it has to pass. It is true, that there is some variation in the size of the head; but these are exceptions, and the computation must be made on the average size. (See Table, page 36.) The development of the infant's head continues to increase during its sojourn in the uterus; and, therefore, the labour should be ended as near as possible to the time we had fixed for its completion, as there is some doubt how soon effective uterine contraction may ensue after means have been employed to induce it. It would, therefore, be most desirable to commence the operation a few days before the computed period for the fulfilment of labour; especially so when some of the measures are adopted for this purpose.

So long as the membranes are entire, and the infant is unrestricted in its movement and floating in the liquor amnii, its life is comparatively safe; but, as soon as the water is discharged, it is subject to more hazard, from the compression it must necessarily bear, and especially so if the os uteri be not dilated. If this be true in ordinary labour, it is more decidedly so when it is artificially induced. Besides, there is no other means so effectual in distending the cervix, and in dilating the os uteri, as the membranous bag filled with the liquor amnii, which acts during each pain as a powerful wedge.

If the infant should happen to lie in a bad posisition, and require turning, either the old operation or the internal and external manipulation (Dr. Hicks's method) could be undertaken with more ease to the practitioner, and with greater safety to the infant.

On these grounds, then, it is of the greatest importance, when labour is artificially brought on, that the membranes should, if possible, be kept entire; and, therefore, those means should be employed which are calculated to accomplish this object.

There are various measures proposed to induce premature labour, which I shall very briefly mention. Stimulant injections thrown into the rectum, and abdominal frictions, and the application of a firm bandage round the abdomen, etc., ought only to be considered as aiding others.

Secale cornutum, in repeated doses, has been prescribed; but, from its well-known poisonous effects on the infant, it ought never to be employed in these cases.

The old, and perhaps the most common method of puncturing the membranes, is certain in its effects, although some days frequently elapse before labour ensues. Although I have formerly frequently adopted this plan, yet it is objectionable, on account of depriving the infant of the protective influence of the amnion fluid, etc. To partly obviate this evil, it has been proposed to carry an instrument through the os uteri and upwards between the uterus and the membranes, before piercing them.

Dr. Hamilton passed his finger through the os and upwards between the membranes and the uterus, and then round so as to detach
them; and had the utmost confidence in it. His success was great.
" Of forty-six infants thus prematurely brought into the world,
forty-two were born alive." Although this method is safer than the
older for the infant, several days sometimes elapse before uterine
contraction is excited.

The vaginal douche has the confidence of many obstetricians. It
consists of a forcible and continuous stream of water, sometimes
warm and sometimes cold, being directed against the os uteri, so as
to wash out the mucous plug. Although this is comparatively a safe
measure, it is not always certain in its effects, and is also somewhat
slow in acting.

The uterine douche, or injecting water into the uterine cavity by
means of a syringe and an elastic tube passed between the membranes
and uterus, has the approval of some practitioners. A considerable
quantity of fluid has been thrown up by some; but this is a most
hazardous experiment. Others have only injected three or four
ounces. The risk of separating the placenta and throwing air into
the uterine vessels renders the uterine douche rather objectionable.

Mechanical dilatation of the os by expanding instruments has
been recommended; but such a plan ought never to be done; it is
attended with great hazard.

Sponges, prepared so as to easily pass through the os, and left to
expand, are comparatively safe, and may sometimes be employed as
preparative measures. Distending the vagina with sponge-plugs, or
by the introduction of a bladder which is afterwards filled by a
syringe with water. One formed of caoutchouc is better adapted
for the purpose. These latter methods are useful, precursory to
other plans.

Elastic bags of various sizes have been contrived by Dr. Barnes,
which are to be distended with water when they have been passed
through the os uteri. As dilators, these contrivances are both safer
and more efficacious.

The attempts to dilate the os uteri should be both gentle and
gradual, and made to resemble as nearly as possible the method
Nature pursues in opening this part. Forcible dilatation, without
preparation, is at all times most mischievous. In cases of labour in
which the hand has to be introduced through the os uteri, this operation ought not to be undertaken until this part (the os) becomes

dilatable. So, in the operation of the induction of premature labour, our efforts ought to be directed to attain, if possible, this state.

In December 1844, I proposed galvanism as an important means of arresting uterine hæmorrhage, and I also at the same time recommended this agency for the induction of premature labour; and my opinion still remains the same. If, however, galvanism is not used to excite uterine action *de novo* in these cases, its employment will be found most advantageous when uterine contraction does not easily or vigorously respond to the employment of some of the other measures. (*Provincial Medical and Surgical Journal*, Dec. 1844.)

Whatever plan is adopted, we should never forget what has been before said as to the necessity of having the parturient process completed as nearly as possible within the period of pregnancy fixed for its accomplishment.

CHAPTER VII.

The Means of Delivery by Destructive Operations.

I.—*The Induction of Abortion.* The induction of abortion has been proposed for the purpose of superseding the necessity of the Cæsarean section; but, in general, the woman has passed the period when it could be advantageously performed. In the great majority of such cases, she has arrived at the full period of pregnancy, and in many cases labour has actually commenced before the obstetrician has become acquainted with the malconformation of the pelvis. Sometimes he becomes acquainted with the pelvic deformity from the difficulty he has experienced in a former labour. It occasionally occurs, although very seldom, that the presumptive evidence of a malformed pelvis may be so strikingly observable in the early months of a first pregnancy as to induce the woman or her friends to apply to an obstetrician. But tumours of different kinds and exostosis may exist in the pelvis, without affording any indications whatever which might lead to a suspicion of their existence.

Whenever it is ascertained, after a most careful investigation in a first pregnancy, that the pelvic capacity is either positively or relatively too small to permit a viable infant to pass, then it would be justifiable, if possible, to perform this operation. But, if the woman again become pregnant, a question arises, whether it is justifiable again to adopt this plan. My opinion (which I submit with great deference to the profession) is, that it ought not a second time to be performed. If such a practice be admitted as sound, it establishes a principle totally at variance with the laws of God and man. The remarks to be made hereafter on the comparative value of maternal and fœtal life will, I hope, be fully considered before such steps are a second time followed.

It has been remarked, that some teachers of midwifery in this country have asserted that this operation should be only once performed, after which the wretched woman should be left to take the fearful chance of the Cæsarean section. To say this, was to assume the position of the Supreme Judge. Just as well we ought to cure syphilis once only. It is said to be "a moral dogma, absurd and immoral, to prefer an ovum of four or five months, dependent for its existence on the mother." I shall not attempt to refute these remarks; but, after I have fully put my opinions before the profession, I shall content myself to leave the subject in their hands, with a desire that they will carefully weigh all the contingent circumstances, and consider whether there is any validity in my observations.

It is not on moral grounds alone that I object to the induction of abortion in order to supersede (as it is said) the Cæsarean section. It is not so safe an operation as it is usually represented. On the contrary, sometimes great danger has succeeded, and in some cases even death has ensued. Great difficulty has frequently been experienced in its performance, and in some cases it could not be accomplished. When the pelvis is highly distorted by mollities ossium, its entire character is changed; its cavity becomes altered in its shape, and all its diameters are very much diminished, whilst the depth anteriorly is very considerably increased. The position of the viscera which are normally contained within the pelvis is changed according to the degree of distortion. The uterus is especially altered in its relative position; it stands obliquely above the brim; and, in most cases of extreme deformity, the os uteri cannot be felt. (See preceding remarks.) Under such circumstances, it is utterly impossible to perform this operation; and, in many cases, great risk is incurred by making the attempt. It is true that, by rash and rude manœuvres, so much mischief may be done that the expulsion of the ovum follows, although there has been no direct entrance into the os uteri, but solely in consequence of the injury inflicted upon the uterus or upon some contiguous organs, which is succeeded by great constitutional irritation, fever, etc., and sometimes by death. An experienced practitioner unsuccessfully attempted to destroy the ovum. The woman died from the effects. The pelvis is in my possession, and. is an example of very great distortion from mollities ossium. Similar cases are also elsewhere recorded. In pelves distorted from the effects of rickets, in which the brim is elliptical, and the cavity and outlet comparatively more capacious, the difficulties above mentioned would be found considerably less.

I may be told that the difficulties and risks of attempting to induce abortion by passing an instrument through the os uteri, for the purpose of destroying the ovum, may be almost altogether avoided by the employment of the douche. From all the information which I have been able to obtain upon this subject, this measure has very frequently failed to produce any effect when employed in the early months of pregnancy.

II.—*Craniotomy.* Craniotomy is recognised in these kingdoms as an operation of election, and is most extensively and frequently performed. It is employed in those cases of difficult labours in which the women cannot be delivered by the forceps, long or short, by the vectis, or by turning. It is also often had recourse to in many contingent accidents which happen during parturition, as in some cases of accidental and unavoidable hæmorrhage, in some cases of convulsions, in some cases of rupture of the uterus, and also in those cases of protracted labours in which, from the neglect or ignorance of the practitioner, the pelvic organs and tissues are brought into such a state from pressure as to render delivery by other means hazardous to the life of the woman.

It has been proposed in cases of osseous deposits in the pelvis, on the grounds that it is impossible to estimate their density, and that most likely the structure would yield or even break down under the pressure made upon it during the extraction of the reduced head. This is, however, an unwise proposition, and ought not to be entertained upon such a presumption alone.

Now, when we contemplate the aggregate amount of infants destroyed by craniotomy in these countries for one year, the thought must be truly appalling. The facts of such a case cannot be, unfortunately, accurately arrived at. Reports of lying-in hospitals may in some degree show the force of this remark. Dr. Collins reports that, during his mastership at the Dublin Lying-in Hospital, 16,414 women were delivered, during which time craniotomy was performed in seventy-nine cases. Dr. Joseph Clarke reports that, in 10,387 cases of labour, craniotomy had been performed forty-nine times.

Now, assuming, in the first place, that craniotomy was performed relatively as frequently in the aggregate amount of labours in England and Wales which occurred in one year, as it was under Dr. Clarke's management in the aggregate of his cases, we should have 2,834½ infants annually destroyed by this operation; and, by making a similar relative computation of Dr. Collins's cases, there would be 2,887¾ infants destroyed in one year. But, if a true statement could be obtained of the number of craniotomy operations which are annually performed in these kingdoms, the aggregate amount would far exceed either those of Dr. Clarke or those of Dr. Collins.

As it is so difficult—nay, I would say, quite impossible—to ascertain with arithmetical accuracy the real condition of the apertures and the cavity of the pelvis, we ought, in all cases of slighter degrees of distortion, as far as possible, to endeavour to save the infant, by first making a cautious and judicious trial of the forceps or turning, before we have recourse to craniotomy.

Then, as we have craniotomy performed in all cases in which the pelvic apertures or its cavity are either relatively or positively diminished, so as not to allow delivery by other means; as we know that most of the obstructing causes to labours progressively increase in size,—it must be evident that craniotomy must be much more difficult and dangerous to perform in some cases than it is in others. On this account, I shall treat of it under two heads.

The first division includes those cases in which there is relatively no very great disproportion between the pelvic measurements and those of the head of the infant. In some of these cases, the mere perforation of the skull will suffice to set it free. In others, it will also be necessary to break up the brain, and then either partially or entirely to remove it from the cranial cavity; after which, it may be expelled by the uterus, or drawn out by the hand alone, or by the aid of the crotchet, or by that of the craniotomy-forceps.

The second division embraces those cases in which there is relatively greater disproportion between the pelvis and the infant's head. There is, however, even in these cases, more difficulty experienced, and more danger attending the operation, in some than is found in others.

The pelvis may be distorted by malacosteon or rickets, or its cavity may be so much diminished by exostosis or tumours that a question may arise whether a mutilated child can pass through it. The opinions of different writers vary as to the space necessary to exist in the pelvis in order that a craniotomised infant can be dragged through it. Some state that a free space of one inch and a half in the antero-posterior diameter of the pelvis is quite sufficient; others say an inch and three-quarters is required; whilst others, again, affirm that, unless there be a space equal to two inches in this diameter, a mutilated infant cannot be drawn through the pelvis. One writer, however, has had the boldness to declare that he has delivered a woman when there was only one inch and a quarter space in the antero-posterior diameter.

These discrepancies of opinion as to the required space for crotchet-delivery are difficult to understand; but the different characters which pelves assume may in a measure account for them. But there has, doubtless, been some mistake made in either the accuracy of the measurement or in the age and development of the infant, as it is quite impossible to deliver a full-grown infant when such a contraction of the pelvis exists as the minimum above mentioned. There is an unchangeable mechanical law which cannot be averted in these cases; that is, a body of a definite or given size cannot be drawn through an opening whose diameters are less than itself. Then, in order to reduce the infant's head, the vaulted part of it must be removed by taking away the two parietal and the frontal bones. Dr. Osborne reduced the head of the infant as far as possible, and then placed the base in (as he thought) the most favourable position by turning it so as to bring it sideways first through the pelvis. He succeeded after great efforts, and delivered the woman, whose pelvis measured at the brim, in its antero-posterior diameter, only (as he says) one inch and a half. Dr. Osborne was doubtless mistaken in his conclusions, which has been so ably and clearly proved by Dr. Hull and Dr. A. Hamilton.

The measurement of the side of the base of the skull corresponds with Dr. Osborne's estimation of it; but, in his anxiety to astonish the profession, and to prove his great achievement, he overlooked the fact that the other side of the head had to follow; and that the bulk must, therefore, be necessarily greatly increased by the addition of the cervical vertebræ and the soft part of the infant's neck, which must lie upon it and pass at the same time.

Now Dr. Hull has experimentally and indisputably proved the fallacy of this assertion; and has shown that the least measurement of the head, when it has been reduced to the utmost, after dragging away the frontal and the two parietal bones, is from the root of the nose to the chin; and, therefore, in order to bring the head (after craniotomy) through the smallest possible pelvic space, the face must be brought first. Dr. Hull, in Plate xii, Fig. 1 (*Observations*, etc.), gives a representation of the reduced head, placed over a sketch of the brim of a distorted pelvis; as well as the outline of that of

Eliz. Sherwood. So that, in such cases, it is most desirable to convert the case from a vertex, if that were the original presentation, to a face case. After this change has been accomplished, the crotchet should be fixed in that situation, so as to turn the chin towards the pubes; and the extractive force should be directed so as to draw down and keep the chin in the anterior part of the pelvis, as the natural flexion of the head with the vertebræ facilitates the passage of the chin under the arch of the pubes. Great care should be taken to prevent injury being done to the uterus or the vagina by the sharp edges or points of the bones of the skull, by placing over them the scalp-integuments.

Dr. Davis says the necessity for Cæsarean section may be reduced to zero by craniotomy; and, using his osteotomist, he asserts that he has succeeded in bringing the reduced skull of the infant through the space existing in the pelvis of Elizabeth Thompson.

This operation was undertaken on a block of wood, in which the pelvis was carved, etc. I had (now in St. Mary's Hospital) similar blocks; but I could never accomplish the extraction. However, it is one thing to operate on an inanimate machine, however accurately formed, and another to operate in the pelvis of a living woman. I had different preparations made of the base of the cranium, with the vertebræ lying over the side and over the occiput, to show their relative measurement to the brims of different sized pelves, which were cut in wood.

But a practical question suggests itself : Will the performance of craniotomy meet all the difficulties arising from distortions of the pelvis ? or can a woman be delivered by this operation, however greatly contracted the brim of the pelvis may be ? Notwithstanding the great reduction which may be made in the head of the infant, and however favourably its base may be placed, I most unhesitatingly assert that it is sometimes utterly impossible by any means whatever, either by the use of the osteotomist or of the cephalatribe, to deliver the woman. We ought never to disguise from ourselves that, in a great number of cases of extreme distortion, it is not possible to attempt delivery, as neither the os uteri nor the presentation of the infant can possibly be felt. This was found to be the case in many of the women whose cases are tabulated. (*Vide* remarks on the necessity.)

But, in many cases in which this information has been obtained, the head of the infant has been opened, and in some instances it has been reduced to its utmost limits, and yet the practitioner has been unable to drag it through the pelvis. Dr. Hull states in his *Defence* (p. 222) that ten women, upon whom embryulcia had been performed, lost their lives. He also relates three other cases, in which both the mothers and the infants perished. In one, neither the os uteri nor presentation could be reached; the uterus ruptured, and the infant escaped into the abdominal cavity. In another, after great difficulty, the breech was found to present. An attempt was made to pass the hand to lay hold of this part; but it failed, on account of the great pelvic contraction. After a second trial, the blunt hook was with great difficulty fixed; but, "notwithstanding all my exertions, the presentation could not be brought lower than the brim of the pelvis." She, therefore, died undelivered. In the third case, Ellen Gyte, who had been in labour sixty hours, the head was opened, and the crotchet applied; but, after the most strenuous exertions, it could not be brought through the pelvis. The vagina ruptured, and the infant escaped into the abdominal cavity. The pelvis was highly distorted; the diameter of the largest circle that could be formed in the superior aperture was two inches and one-twelfth. The pelvis now belongs to me.

In a case in which the pelvis was highly distorted, under the care of the late Mr. R——, the head was perforated; but, after the most powerful efforts, he was unable to bring it down. The uterus ruptured, and the child escaped into the abdomen. She died undelivered. A cast of the pelvis is in my possession. The cause of distortion in all these cases was mollities ossium. I have known several other cases in which the same melancholy events happened; and doubtless, if the grave could unfold the mysteries contained within it, very many more horrible terminations of pregnancy would be brought to light.

But, even granting that, in some extreme cases of distortion, there may exist sufficient pelvic space to permit an infant, whose head has been reduced to the utmost, to be dragged by great force through the pelvis, yet it must not be forgotten that such an operation must be extremely hazardous to the life of the mother. It is one thing to deliver the woman, and another to do so safely. It is much to be deplored, that this operation is still permitted to be so unconditionally performed; especially so when the injuries which are frequently inflicted on the pelvic organs, and when its comparative mortality, are considered.

The statistics of craniotomy are in a very unsatisfactory state. After a very minute search, I have been quite unable to draw out such tables as I wished. Feeling strongly the importance of deductions which are to be drawn from an accumulation of well authenticated facts, I published a letter (*Provincial Medical and Surgical Journal*, vol. xviii, p. 494, 1849) requesting that the members of the Association would transmit me a statement of all the cases which had happened in each of their practices; but my appeal did not elicit much information. Not having been successful in this attempt, I could only avail myself of the statements already published by my worthy and esteemed friend Dr. Churchill of Dublin, in his *Theory and Practice of Midwifery*. The following is a copy of his tables.

Authors.	No. of cases.	Mothers died.
Dr. Smellie	44	4
Mr. Perfect	3	0
Dr. Joseph Clarke	49	16
Dr. Granville	3	3
Dr. Ramsbotham	34	5
Dr. Maunsell	5	2
Mr. Gregory	2	1
Dr. Collins	79	15
Dr. McClintock } Dr. Hardy }	52	8
Dr. Beatty	3	0
Dr. Churchill	11	1
Mr. Warrington	1	0
	286	55

Or about 1 in 5.

" Independently of the abuse of this operation (craniotomy)—of its unjustifiable frequency—let us for a moment look at its relative fatality, when compared with the Cæsarean section.

" According to the above" (Dr. Churchill's) " statistics, British practitioners resort to craniotomy once in 219 cases; the French, once in 1,205⅔ cases; the Germans, once in 1,944⅓. The average, therefore, of these three nations, will be one in 896½. In 252 cases, 50 mothers died, or about one in every five. As regards the Cæsarean section, the same author states that he has collected 321 operations since 1750, from which 149 mothers recovered; and in 187 cases, where the result is mentioned, 130 children were saved, and 57 lost.

" Hence, then, we have a calculation showing that in craniotomy, where of necessity all the children must be sacrificed, one woman out of every five died; while, in the Cæsarean section, one mother recovered out of two and a fraction, and the success to the child was certainly most fortunate."

The destruction by craniotomy of a number of infants in different women, in successive labours, both in the practice of other obstetricians, as well as those which happened to myself; the ignorant and groundless adoption of this operation; the unprofessional and disgraceful manner in which I have known it performed (in one case, the head was opened by a pair of scissors, which were obtained from some part of the family; in another case, by a penknife); and the operation being frequently performed without a consultation,—these circumstances, and deep reflection on the social and moral right to destroy life, convinced me that the present recognised practice in these cases ought to be modified.

In a course of lectures delivered to the members of the profession, I strongly denounced craniotomy as an operation of election; and I recommended it to be performed generally as an operation of necessity, and that it should only be conditionally accepted as one of election. These opinions I then expressed, and have ever since advocated and in every way promulgated. (*Provincial Medical and Surgical Journal*, and *British Obstetric Record*, etc.)

Such, then, was my proposition in 1843; and now, in 1865, after long reflection and matured experience, I am, if possible, more strengthened in my convictions. The remarks of Dr. Bedford, which I afterwards found in his translation of Chailly, bear so forcibly upon the subject, that I do not hesitate to quote them. He says:

" The Cæsarean section is undoubtedly a dread alternative for the accoucheur to choose; but I cannot agree with Dr. Chailly, that its fatality is so great as he represents; nor am I disposed to adopt the opinion (unfortunately too general) that craniotomy is always to be preferred to the Cæsarean section. In truth, it needs some nerve, and, for a man of high moral feeling, much evidence as to the necessity of the operation, before he can bring himself to the perpetration of an act which requires, for his own peace of mind, the fullest justification. The man who would wantonly thrust an instrument of death into the brain of a living fœtus would not scruple, under the mantle of night, to use the stiletto of the assassin; yet how often has the fœtus been recklessly torn from its mother's

womb piecemeal, and its fragments held up to the contemplation of
the astonished and ignorant spectators as a testimony undoubted of
the operator's skill.   Oh! could the grave speak, how eloquent,
how momentous, how damning to the character of those who specu-
late in human life, would be its revelations !"

The facility of its peformance has led to its abuse.   Its recognition
in the British obstetric code reflects no credit on the country, especially when its frequent performance is compared with the practice
in France and Germany.   It cannot be denied that craniotomy is a
cruel operation ; for surely no obstetrician ought to be so ignorant as
to suppose that the infant *in utero* is void of sensibility.   Yet there
are some parties (if judged by their estimate of its life) who either
professedly or actually believe it does not feel.   This is, however,
either a moral or a physiological fallacy ; for there is not a doubt
that it is endowed with this faculty in a very eminent degree, and
consequently it must endure great bodily suffering from this practice.
There are some practitioners who admit the existence of this principle ; and, with the view of avoiding the infliction of pain caused
by the perforator, delay opening the head until after its death.
Craniotomy and embryotomy are the only operations which are
recognised and justified by the British profession for the purpose of
destroying life ; but, although they are admitted into our obstetric
code, they are not to be found in that of the law, and are only
sanctioned by custom, and, through this usage, considered as " justifiable homicide".

There is no difficulty in understanding why so low an estimate of
fœtal life is entertained, when we consider what the doctrine is which
is taught *in cathedrâ* and *extra cathedram*—" that, to save the life of
the mother, it is justifiable to destroy the infant." From the early
inculcation of this principle, the student becomes hardened to the
performance of this dreadful task, and does it without compunction,
and, no doubt, sometimes without reflection.   My experience war-
rants me to make the above declaration, having met with many cases
in which this operation has been most unnecessarily, and in some
cases has been most unprofessionally, nay, most unjustifiably, performed.

Having now very fully expressed my objections to the recognition
of craniotomy as an operation of election, I shall proceed to state
my opinion in what cases it might be considered right to perform it.

When the infant is ascertained by the stethoscope to be dead, and the time for delivery has arrived, then craniotomy is justifiable; but the labour ought never to proceed a moment longer after delivery is required, in expectation of this event happening. The destruction of the infant from procrastination differs very little in principle from taking its life by the perforator; and, therefore, timely and other appropriate measures should be employed to prevent this event. Such are the long and short forceps, turning, and the Cæsarean section.

When some serious accident happens, such as rupture of the uterus, it would sometimes be admissible to perforate the head; and little compunction need be felt, as the infant is nearly if not always dead.

In a first labour, in which the pelvic cavity is so diminished that a mature unmutilated infant cannot be delivered, and also in those cases in which this mischief has taken place after the woman has naturally borne one or more children, the operation may be performed.

Embryotomy is justifiable in cases in which turning is quite impracticable. In these cases, the infant is nearly always dead.

In some cases of protracted labour, in which the pelvic organs or tissues have already sustained such great injury from pressure, and in which it would be extremely hazardous to the woman's life to deliver with the forceps, embryotomy may be practised. This event, however, will seldom or never happen in the hands of a judicious practitioner.

In some cases of hydrocephalic enlargement of the head, its size must be diminished by letting out the water by means of the perforator, or by a trocar. If this latter instrument can be successfully used, it is to be preferred.

CHAPTER VIII.

Symphyseotomy and Mechanical Dilatation.

I HAVE now to speak of two propositions intended to supersede the Cæsarean section, and which cannot be included under either of the former divisions.

I.—*Symphyseotomy.* Symphyseotomy, or a division of the cartilages constituting the symphysis pubis, was advocated by Sigault, and his suggestion was received with enthusiastic approval. A medal was struck off in honour of him.

British obstetricians have discountenanced this operation, because it is not only inadequate to increase the diameters of the pelvis, so as in any way to facilitate delivery when this bony cavity is so contracted as to require the Cæsarean section, but because it would be attended by most dangerous results.

British medical literature has only once been disgraced by the record of the performance of this operation. I have already adverted to Mr. Simmons's proposed compound operation of symphyseotomy and craniotomy.

II.—*Mechanical Dilatation of the Pelvis.* At a late discussion on a case of Cæsarean section at the Royal Medical and Chirurgical Society, which was reported in the *Lancet*, it was stated that a pelvis which was distorted from mollities ossium might be dilated by means of bags introduced within its cavity, and distended by either water or air. It was asserted, that this practice had been adopted in one case with the effect of widening the pelvic space. The President stated that he had found the bones affected with this disease yield during the extraction of the child after craniotomy.

From my own practical knowledge, I can truly affirm the truth of the last statement. Some years ago, I made the fact known to the profession.

In a case, at some distance from Manchester, in which the pelvic space at the brim was about two inches and a quarter, it was deemed right to craniotomise the child. After fixing the crotchet, and adjusting the head in the most favourable position, force was cautiously used, and, after a few extractive efforts had been made, the head gradually descended, during which time the pelvic bones yielded to the pressure, and ultimately delivery was accomplished. Immediately afterwards the pelvis was examined, and found to have regained its former dimensions.

Other cases of this kind have come within my knowledge. One of great interest is briefly related in the *Provincial Med. and Surg. Journ.*, vol. ii, page 706, 1847. Although it is true that the pelvic bones, when affected with mollities ossium, do sometimes yield to the pressure of the child when drawn through the cavity; and although the pelvis, as before mentioned, may be partially dilated by the mechanical influence of the elastic bag, yet, in my opinion, practical rules cannot be based on such an uncertain event where life is concerned.

Before such a change can be safely effected, a very considerable and an uniform softening must have taken place in the greater number, if not in all, the bones of the pelvis which are subjected to the influence of pressure, whether it be produced by the child or by artificial means. We know very well that this uniform change is found to happen in very few cases. Some of the bones sometimes become very soft, whilst others are comparatively unchanged. In other cases, some of the bones become very soft; whilst others become very hard and brittle. Sometimes, the pelvis becomes very highly distorted, and all its bones are extremely brittle and fragile, as happened in Dr. Murphy's case.

In a pelvis thus changed by disease, what would be the result (supposing it possible to accomplish it) of dragging a full grown mutilated child through its cavity, or of attempting, by artificial and mechanical force, to dilate the pelvis for the purpose of accomplishing the delivery? The bones must be smashed, or at least so much broken, that irreparable injury must be produced. Even assuming that the bones are so uniformly softened as to yield to the pressure, it is quite certain that the increased capacity would only be temporary, as the bones would immediately and most likely completely return to their former position as soon as the pressure was removed.

CHAPTER IX.

The Comparative Value of Maternal and Infantile Life.

THE British obstetric principle, which admits the preferential use of the crotchet, or the induction of abortion, is based on a calculation made as to the relative value of the life of the mother and of that of the infant or of the embryo.

It is said, and no doubt truly, that the social relations of the woman are greater than those of the infant. She is endeared to her husband, it may be to her children, and perhaps to her brothers and sisters, besides other kindred and friends. In the abstract, these are weighty considerations, and are calculated to bring conviction to the mind, that her claims for the preservation of life greatly preponderate over those of the infant or of the embryo. It may be stated that these beings are unequal to the mother in organisation, having no moral or religious responsibility, no social ties, no anticipation of their future doom ; and further, as regards the latter (the embryo), that it is at the very time drawing its nourishment from the mother's existence, that it has never had a distinct or separate life, and that it is little more than a member of the mother. These arguments, when only abstractedly considered, appear to be true ; and to warrant the deduction that the life of the infant or embryo is of little value when compared with that of the mother.

The impulse of natural feeling would probably—nay, nearly to a certainty—induce a man to decide in favour of this proposition. But, in the settlement of a question which involves the preservation or destruction of a human being, neither abstract reasoning nor feeling should be allowed to influence the obstetrician ;—conscience, reason, and judgment, ought to actuate him, after having fully and deliberately considered all the relative and contingent circumstances which either now or in future appertain to the case.

The unfounded and unwise opinions of Dr. Osborne primarily and

mainly led a large section of the profession to estimate the life of
the infant *in utero* at a very low value. He considered it nearly
as a nonentity; as devoid of sensation, and also as nearly deprived
of motion. But I think I am asserting the truth when I say that
there are few, if any, members of our profession who now entertain
such opinions.

According to British practice, the destruction of the infant is not
limited to one; but if the cause which required its sacrifice in the
first instance be permanent, then in each successive labour, no matter
what number, the same operation must be performed. Hence in the
end there must be a fearful sacrifice of human life.

The repeated necessity of craniotomy in the same woman demands
from the obstetrician serious consideration. In some cases, from one
to twelve infants have been destroyed. Can such a procedure be
justifiable? The obstetrician should pause; he should reflect. It is
a dreadful position to be placed in, to have one's hands imbrued with
innocent blood.

The woman is *ipso facto* one party, and indeed the chief party,
who has brought into existence the innocent being whose life the
practitioner is employed to take away. It may be argued, as a plea
for her justification, that the wife is subject to her husband; and
there can be no doubt that she has engaged to be so in the matri-
monial contract, which was mutual. But if it be considered right
(which in such a case as this could only be so conditionally) strictly
to observe this promise, it must be equally imperative upon both
parties to obey the law of nature and fulfil their mutual pledge
to procreate (and without doubt preserve) the species, both of which
vows are broken by the employment of the crotchet.

It may again be urged, that both the parties were alike ignorant
of any cause (otherwise they were solemnly called upon at the altar
to avow it) which would interfere with the great object of matri-
mony. Therefore, the woman, unacquainted with her physical
organic defect, would be entitled to have those measures adopted for
her first delivery which would expose her life to the least hazard.
Although the comparative safety of delivery by the only two available methods is unsettled by either positive or correct statistical
evidence, yet, if she or her husband desire that craniotomy should be
performed, then the obstetrician would probably act correctly in
performing it.

But, in a second pregnancy, when they are fully acquainted that an unmutilated infant cannot be born, the question stands on very different social and moral grounds. The practitioner is here placed in a most responsible and trying position when called upon to decide whether he ought, time after time, or thus repeatedly, be made the agent to take away life. I entertain the fullest conviction that a great proportion of our profession have most conscientious scruples to repeat this revolting operation in the same woman. This destruction of infants, in my humble opinion, can be justified on no principle, and is only sanctioned by the dogma of the schools or by usage.

Dr. Denman had aversions to repeated crotchet-operations. He says: "Suppose, for instance, a woman, married, who was so unfortunately framed that she could not possibly bear a living child by any method hitherto known. The first time of her being in labour, no reasonable man could hesitate to afford relief at the expense of the child. Even a second or a third trial might be justifiable to ascertain the fact of the impossibility." This eminent writer most decidedly erred in even conditionally sanctioning a repetition of this operation. In such cases, the impossibility of delivery of an unmutilated infant *per vias naturales* can and ought to be proved by a single case as clearly as by twenty, and when so shown, the Cæsarean section should be performed.

It is by no means to be understood that the life of the infant must never be sacrificed to save the mother. On the contrary, I have already enumerated cases in which craniotomy ought to be performed as an operation of election; but it is not right to destroy the infant on the unfounded assumption that the mother could alone be saved by it; a deduction altogether untrue, and unsanctioned by statistical evidence.

The life of the woman is not, either relatively or comparatively, always of the same value. If she be afflicted with a serious disease, or labouring under some incurable malady, being unfit and unable to discharge her domestic and her social duties, which performance can alone render her life desirable to herself or to her friends, then, under such circumstances, the infant's life ought not to be sacrificed for the mere ideal chance of prolonging her miserable existence, which is a positive evil to herself.

Again, in our estimate of the comparative value of the two lives, we should especially consider whether the cause of difficulty is temporary only, or permanent. If it be of the latter character, then the infant's life (except as aforesaid conditionally) ought to be considered

I

higher ; and if of the former kind, then we should invariably decide in favour of the mother. The obstetrician should, therefore, endeavour, as far as is compatible with the safety of the mother, to preserve the infant ; for I know no case in which an intention or a desire to sacrifice her can ever be entertained, as the especial object of the practitioner should always be to try to save both lives.

When the contingent hazards of craniotomy, and the risk of its abuse are considered, and as we know that the act is the sacrifice of life, and that this awful catastrophe must be often repeated in order to carry out the abstract proposition " to save the life of the woman by destroying the infant"—when we remember the difficulty which in extreme cases is experienced in performing it, the cruelty it inflicts, and many other evils consequent upon it—we may truly wonder that professional men should allow their minds to be haunted by an imaginary Cæsarean spectre, and be so obscured to their own moral and social responsibility. Why should the obstetrician stand in such an unenviable position, not only as an accessory, but *ipso facto* the agent ? Again, I ask, ought he to be called upon, and ought he to consent, to victimise poor helpless infants in successive pregnancies, in numbers which make one shudder to recount ? Does this remorseless sacrifice of human life correspond with those high moral principles which the members of our noble profession ought to possess ?

The eminent Professor of Midwifery in Edinburgh makes the following pertinent remarks. He says :—" Formerly medical practitioners seem to have thought little, and medical writers said little, regarding the very repulsive and revolting character of the operation of craniotomy, when performed, as it frequently was, when the child was still living. Apparently, some obstetric practitioners and writers of the present day continue to look upon the practice of craniotomy as one that should not unfrequently be adopted, and one which it is quite justifiable to adopt. Obstetric reports and collections of cases have been published within the last few years describing craniotomy as performed forty or fifty times, or oftener, by the hand of the same practitioner. But, perhaps, ere long, it will become a question in professional ethics, whether a professional man is, under the name of a so-called operation, justified in deliberately destroying the life of a living human being."

Woman naturally is mild, kind, and humane. She is endowed with great fortitude and undaunted courage. She has generally a great desire for offspring, and has a great love for children. Then how can we suppose that any woman with a well regulated mind, if fully aware of her responsibility, could willingly be a consenting party to the repeated destruction of her unborn infants? According to my own knowledge, the case is otherwise. I feel convinced in my own mind that there would scarcely be a woman to be found, who would not suffer any amount of bodily pain to save her infant.

Every woman in whom there exists organic impediment to the passage of a mature or full-grown infant, ought to be at proper time fully informed of the nature and as to the degree of the obstacle. She should also be made acquainted with the alternative operations which are suitable to meet her case. If the obstruction be moderate in degree, then the forceps, turning, or the induction of premature labour, will be proper; but if these means are not available, or if the cause of difficulty is great in degree, then the performance of the Cæsarean section will be required.

CHAPTER X

Considerations on the Cæsarean Section as an Operation of Election.

In the preceding remarks, I have to my own mind most satisfactorily proved that the Cæsarean section is at least an operation of necessity, and that those measures which have been proposed as substitutes are totally inadequate to supersede it.

The (British) statistics of this operation are most certainly unfavourable; yet it has, I think, been shewn that the great cause of the maternal mortality is avoidable; and that most of the other alleged causes of this fatality have been pointed out to be subject to control, and that some of them are really preventable, whilst others are remediable.

Although the deaths of the women from this operation, as hitherto performed, are very numerous, yet objections ought not to be raised against it on data so unsatisfactory as those are which now influence the opinions of British practitioners. When I speak of unsatisfactory data, I mean that we should not take an abstract view of them, and attach to them more importance than they deserve. British obstetricians have been guided more from prejudice arising from preconceived opinions, than from an analysis of the real causes of death in these cases.

A comparative estimate of the mortality between this operation and craniotomy has never been fairly made. As regards the Cæsarean section, all the deaths are known, whereas those of craniotomy are only very partially known. This latter operation is not confined to any particular class of cases, but it is performed under very different circumstances and dangers—in some cases of accidents which occur in labours, such as hæmorrhage, convulsion, and other contingent mischief, which happen in women whose constitutional powers are unimpaired; whilst the greater part of the women who have undergone the Cæsarean section have laboured under incurable disease, and have had additional injury inflicted upon them by protraction, and in many cases by the practitioner in his ineffectual performance of craniotomy, etc.

Dr. Joseph Clarke reports 49 cases of craniotomy, in which 16 mothers died, or one in three. Dr. Collins performed craniotomy in 79 cases, in which 15 died, or one in five. Now, in Dr. Clarke's practice collectively, there are recorded 65 deaths;* in Dr. Collins's practice collectively, there are recorded 94 deaths.* Thus the statistics of craniotomy, which are indiscriminately made up of all kinds of cases in which it has been performed, show an unfavourable result.

Besides this, we have no account of the injuries which are inflicted on the pelvic organs by the instrument used in this operation.

In 77 cases of Cæsarean section, there were collectively 98 deaths,* the greater portion of which were not due to the operation; but, on the contrary, very many lives might have been saved, if it had been timely and judiciously performed.

Notwithstanding all the preexisting dangers in Cæsarean cases, several recoveries have taken place. These favourable terminations ought to encourage us to hope, and indeed ought to inspire us with confidence, that if the operation were earlier performed, and on a different class of subjects, it would be attended with infinitely more success.

These cases prove that, notwithstanding the serious nature of the constitutional disease which existed in these women, the vital powers were equal to the reparation of both the abdominal and uterine incisions; and also show the fallacy of the opinion that wounds of the uterus are necessarily mortal. The conservative vital powers were wonderfully apparent in the case of Mrs. Sankey, which is related in the *London Medical Gazette*, also in the *Provincial Medical and Surgical Journal*. The restorative powers in this individual were really so active as to impress my mind with the conviction that the chance of success would be as great in well conducted Cæsarean cases as that which attends other capital operations.

Another woman (Mrs. Haigh), in whom mollities ossium existed to a great extent, and whose pelvis was very much distorted, showed great restorative powers. She recovered, and lived several years

---

* These accounts contain the number of deaths of both women and infants.

afterwards. She died exhausted by the disease. *Post mortem* examination revealed no disease in the abdominal or pelvic viscera. The uterine tissue was uniform in appearance, there being no cicatrix to indicate the site of the incision. There was only a single band of lymph, not thicker than a thread, passing from this organ to the peritoneum; so that there existed no mechanical obstacle to the distension and ascent of the uterus, if she had unfortunately become pregnant again; but the moral rule of abstinence prevailed with both her and her husband.

Recoveries after rupture of the uterus afford further evidence that wounds of this organ are not always mortal. The lacerated tissue in these cases must be in a very different, and indeed in a much more unfavourable, condition for uniting, than in Cæsarean cases. In these accidents, the peritoneum, the abdominal and the pelvic viscera, must inevitably sustain very great injury by the escape of the infant, and also very frequently of the placenta, through the uterine rent; and also from the attempts which are made for the delivery of the woman. The same mischief cannot possibly be inflicted by a well conducted Cæsarean operation.

Two instances of recovery after rupture of the uterus have occurred in my practice. One of these women became pregnant several times afterwards. In one of these pregnancies, she went to her full time, and bore a child, which is still alive; and she also aborted several times. During her last labour, and also during the several abortive periods, she had the valuable aid and advice of my respected friend Mr. Hunt. Many years afterwards, she died in the Manchester Workhouse. Her body was inspected by Mr. Hunt, in the presence of Dr. Francis and of myself. There was not the slightest trace of the cicatrix in the womb to be seen; but there was a band of slight adhesion to the ilium.

I was consulted by Dr. Clay in his first case of large ovarian tumour, and attended along with him both before, during, and after the operation. I take this opportunity of saying I consider the successful issue of this operation as the commencement of a new era in the history of ovariotomy. It had not been attempted for many years before; and, at the time of its performance, it did not stand as if it were a recognised surgical operation. I attended also along with Dr. Clay many of his next succeeding cases, being present at all the operations. I took great interest in these cases, not only on account of that which necessarily belonged to them, but also because

the results analogically tended to substantiate my views relative to
the probable success of the Cæsarean section.   It is nevertheless
true, that the influence in these two classes of cases is not quite the
same ; yet there is, however, sufficient similarity between them to
lead us to trust more in abdominal surgery.   In ovariotomy, there
is certainly no uterine incision ; but there is a necessary division to be
made of the connecting tissue which exists between the tumour and
the uterus.   In many of these cases, extensive adhesions, which exist
between the tumour and the peritoneum, etc., have to be separated.
It is, however, evident that during the progressive development of
an ovarian tumour, the sympathy of the peritoneum, etc., must in
some measure be blunted, and consequently its susceptibility to mechanical injury must be diminished.

The rest of Dr. Clay's successful cases, and likewise those of Mr.
Spencer Wells, and all those which have occurred to other practitioners, collectively afford strong evidence of the safety of abdominal
incision.

The operations performed by my esteemed friend Dr. Blundell on
animals, to prove some important physiological facts, likewise afford
substantial evidence that abdominal wounds are very much safer
than has been usually considered.

In my introductory remarks, I stated that I should not bring
forward any statistical data, as shown from the result of foreign
cases of the Cæsarean section, although I feel quite sure that the
comparative position of this operation has been damaged by the
omission.   Continental success in this operation has been remarkably
great, when compared with the results of British practice.   There
have been many instances of two or three successful operations on
the same woman.

Having, as I sincerely hope, faithfully and candidly placed all the
circumstances appertaining to the two operations—the Cæsarean
section and craniotomy—before the profession, it now only remains
for me to bring forward my proposition, first made in 1843.   Deep
reflection since that period, and a strong sense of humanity, have
induced me further to declare that the Cæsarean section should be
generally performed as an operation of election ; and that craniotomy
should be as far as possible abolished, and ought only to be performed as an operation of necessity, except (as already adverted to)
in a very few cases.*   I am quite aware that many of the opinions I

* See remarks, pages 51 and 52.

have so urgently stated in the foregoing remarks are at variance with those of the profession generally; yet they have been most conscientiously advocated. They originated from the dictates of humanity, to try to extinguish as far as possible that dreadful expedient—nay, shall I not call it murderous operation?—craniotomy.

Having now fully and without the least reserve put my views into the hands of the profession, I consider I am only doing justice to myself in declaring that I shall not feel called upon to enter into any controversial defence of them.

TABLE OF RECORDED CASES OF CÆSAREAN SECTION IN GREAT BRITAIN AND IRELAND.

No.	Year.	Name and residence of the patient.	By whom and where the case is related.	Operator.	Cause of difficulty.	Duration of the labour.	Mother.		Child.		Mother survived.
							Pre-serv'd	Died	Pre-serv'd	Died	
1	Jan. 9, 1738.	Alice O'Neil, aged 35 years, near Charlemont, Ireland.	Mr. Duncan Stewart, Edinburgh Essays, vol. v, p. 409.	Mary Donnally.	Not stated.	12 days.	P.			D.	
2	June, 1757.	Patterson, Cannon Gate, Edinburgh.	Smellie's Midwifery, vol. iii, coll. 39, No. 2, p. 373.	Mr. Smith.	Distorted pelvis, most likely from mollities ossium.	7 days.		D.		D.	1+ hrs.
3		Not named.	Manuscript Lectures.	Professor Young.	Distorted pelvis, from rickets.	No account.		D.	P.		
4		Not named.	Manuscript Lecture.	Professor Young.	Distorted pelvis, from moll. ossium.	No account.		D.	P.		3 days
5		Not named.	Mentioned in Dr. Hamilton's Outlines of Midwifery.	Mr. Alex. Wood, Edinburgh.	Not stated.	No account.		D.		D.	
6	Before 1740.	Not named, Rochdale, Lancash.	Dr. Hull's Defence, p. 67.	Dr. White, Manchester.	Not stated.	No account.		D.		D.	
7	Oct. 1769.	Martha Rhodes, Loudon.	Dr. Cooper and Mr. Henry Thompson, Lond. Med. Obs. and Inquiries, vol. iv.	Mr. H. Thompson.	Distorted pelvis, from rickets.	Nearly 30 hours.		D.		D.	5 hours
8	1774.	Elizabeth Clerk, aged 30, Edinburgh.	Dr. Alex. Hamilton, Outlines of Midwifery, p. 293.	Mr. W. Chalmers, Edinburgh.	Distorted pelvis, most likely from mollities ossium.	12 days.		D.	P.		26 hrs.
9	August, 1774.	Elizabeth Forster, London.	Dr. Cooper, Lond. Med. Obs. and Inq., vol. v.	Mr. Hunter, London.	Distorted pelvis, from mollities ossium.	60 hours.		D.	P.		25¼ hrs.
10	1775.	Not named.	Dr. Hull's Defence, p. 66.	Mr. W. Whyte, Glasgow.	No account.	No account.		D.		D	No account.
11	1777.	Elizabeth Hutchinson, aged 40, Leicester.	Dr. Vaughan, Cases and Observations on Hydroph.	Mr. Atkinson, Leicester.	Distorted pelvis, from mollities ossium.	Nearly 3 days.		D.	P.		About 60 hrs.
12	Nov. 1793.	Jane Foster, aged 40, Blackrod, Lancashire.	Mr. Barlow, Med. Records and Researches, p. 154; also, his Observations, p. 355.	Mr. Barlow.	Distorted pelvis, from fracture.	5 days.	P.			D.	
13	Sept. 1794.	Isabel Rodman, aged 38, Blackburn.	Dr. Hull's Defence, p. 172.	Dr. Hull.	Distorted pelvis, from mollities ossium.	12 hours.		D.	P.		34 hrs.
14	June, 1795.	Jean Douglas, Edinburgh.	Dr. Alex. Hamilton, Outlines of Midwifery, p. 299.	Dr. James Hamilton, jun.	Distorted pelvis, from mollities ossium.	54 hours. Spurious pains three nights previous.		D.		D.	33 hrs.
15	Sept. 1795.	Anne Lee, Manchester.	Dr. Hull's Defence, p. 162.	Dr. Hull.	Distorted pelvis, from rickets.	10 days.		D.		D.	6 hours
16	1798.	Janet Williamson, aged 38, Kirriemuir, Forfarshire.	Dr. Hull's Defence, p. 188.	Mr. Kay, Forfar.	Distorted pelvis, from mollities ossium.	More than 3 days.		D.		D	11 days
17	June, 1799.	Elizabeth Thompson, aged 39, Hazelhurst, near Ashton-under-Lyne, Lancashire.	Mr. Wm. Wood, London Med. Memoirs, vol. v.	Mr. Wood, Manchester.	Distorted pelvis, from mollities ossium.	21 hours.		D.	P.		76 hrs.
18	March, 1800.	Not named; resided at Edinburgh.	Sir Chas. Bell, Lond. Med.-Chir. Trans., vol. iv.	Mr. Jno. Bell.	Distorted pelvis, from mollities ossium.	Not stated.		D.	P.		Very short time.
19	August, 1801.	Hannah Rheubotham, aged 41, Manchester.	Mr. Wm. Wood, Lond. Med. Phys. Journ., vol. vi, p. 346.	Mr. W. Wood, Manchester.	Distorted pelvis, from mollities ossium.	61 hours.		D.		D.*	24 hrs.
20	Feb. 1801.	Susan Holl, aged 36, Lower Shore, Rochdale, Lancashire.	Dr. Hull's Translation of Baudelocque, p. 154.	Mr. Walter Dunlop.	Distorted pelvis, from mollities ossium.	56 hours.		D.	P.		6 days and 9 hours
21	July, 1811.	Mrs. M., Leith, Scotland.	Dr. Kellie, Ed. Med. and Surg. Journal, vol. viii.	Dr. Kellie.	Distorted pelvis, from mollities ossium.	About 36 hours.		D.	P.		About 24 hrs.
22		Wife of Benjamin Buckley, Staleybridge, Lancashire.	Not before mentioned.	Mr. Hutton.	Distorted pelvis, from mollities ossium.	3 days.		D.		D.	
23		Name unknown; resided at Staleybridge, Lancashire.	Not mentioned before.	Mr. Hutton.	Distorted pelvis, from mollities ossium.	No account as to precise time; but long.		D.	P.		
24	August, 1814.	Wife of Jas. Tinker, aged 34, Moston, Lancashire.	Mr. K. Wood, Med.-Chir. Trans., vol. vii, p. 264.	Mr. K. Wood.	Distorted pelvis, from mollities ossium.	About 40 hours.		D.		D.	10 hrs.
25	Jan. 1817.	Wife of Wm. Ratcliffe, aged 35, Staleybridge, Lancashire.	Not mentioned before.	Mr. Hutton.	Distorted pelvis, from mollities ossium.	No account.		D.	P.		48 hrs.
26 27	July, 1817.	Ann Hacking, aged 42, Blackburn, Lancashire.	Mr. Barlow, Observations, p. 361.	Mr. Barlow.	Distorted pelvis, from mollities ossium.	13 hours.		D.	P.		76 hrs.
	April, 1820.	Mary Ashworth, aged 42, Denton, Lancashire.	Dr. Radford, Edin. Med. & Surg. Jour.; Pros. Med. & Surg. Jour., vol. xv; Lond. Med. Gaz., vol. xlviii, p. 95.	Mr. Morris, Ashton.	Distorted pelvis, from mollities ossium.	37 hours.		D.		D.*	35 hrs.
28	Sept. 1820.	Mrs. Lowe, aged 30, Perth.	Dr. Henderson, Ed. Med. and Surg. Jour., vol. xvii, p. 105.	Dr. Henderson.	Distorted pelvis, from mollities ossium.	102 hours.		D.	P.		20 hrs.
29	April, 1821.	Wife of G. Ridgedale, aged 42, Blackburn, Lancashire.	Mr. Barlow, Observations, p. 375.	Mr. Barlow.	Distorted pelvis, from mollities ossium.	About 84 hours.		D.	P.		52 hrs.

* Dead before operation.

TABLE OF CASES OF CÆSAREAN SECTION (continued).

No.	Year.	Name and residence of the patient.	By whom and where the case is related.	Operator.	Cause of difficulty.	Duration of the labour.	Mother Preserved	Mother Died	Child Preserved	Child Died	Mother survived
30	May, 1821.	Mary Nixon, aged 39, Manchester.	Dr. Radford, Edin. Med. & Surg. Jour.; Lond. Med. Gaz., vol. xlviii, p. 98; Prov. Med. & Sur. Jl., vol. xv, p. 426, 1851.	Mr. Wilson.	Distorted pelvis, from mollities ossium.	22 hours.		D.		D.	67½ hrs.
31	April, 1826.	M. R., aged 22, Stobsmuir, Scotland.	Mr. Crichton, Dundee, Ed. Med. and Surg. Journ., vol. xxx, p. 53.	Mr. Crichton.	Distorted pelvis, from fracture, etc.	6 days.		D.	P.		8 hours.
32	August, 1826.	Mary Forrest, aged 35, three miles from Blackburn, Lancash.	Mr. Barlow, Lond. Med. & Surg. Jour., vol. iv.	Mr. Barlow.	Distorted pelvis, from mollities ossium.	From 30 to 36 hours.		D.	P.		More than 3 days.
33	Sept. 1829.	Mrs. M., aged 26, Belfast.	Communicated by Dr. W. Campbell, Edin. Med. & Surg. Jour., v. xxxv, p. 351.	Dr. M'Kibbin.	Distorted pelvis, from a large exostosis arising from the sacrum.	About 30 hours.		D.		D.+	17 hrs.
34	Nov. 1834.	Mrs. — Dublin.	Dr. Montgomery, Dublin Med. Journ., vol. vi.	Mr. Porter.	Fibrous tumour, growing from substance of uterus and covered by peritoneum.	18 to 20 hours.		D.		D.+	21½ hrs.
35	April, 1834.	Mary Bamford, aged 38, Great Easton, Rockingham.	Mr. T. L. Greaves, Lancet, vol. ii, 1833-4.	Mr. Greaves.	Distorted pelvis, from mollities ossium.	About 34 hours.	P.		P.		
36	May, 1835.	Sarah Date, aged 36, Birmingham.	Mr. Knowles, Trans. Prov. Med. Assoc., vol. iv, p. 376.	Mr. Knowles.	Distorted pelvis, from mollities ossium.	About 30 hours.	P.		P.		
37	Aug. 14, 1840.	Mary Ann Jones, aged 39 Manchester.	Mr. Jas. Whitehead, Manchester, Med. Gaz., vol. xxviii, p. 930, 1840-41.	Mr. Whitehead.	Distorted pelvis, from mollities ossium.	24 hours; in active labour for 2 to 3 hours.	P.		P.		32 days 10 hrs.
38		Name not given, or age; private note, aged 30.	Mr. Dendy, Medical Society of London, Lancet, 1842-43, vol. xliii, p. 691.	Mr. Bryant, Lambeth.	Distorted pelvis, by rickets.	24 hours.		D.		D.	60 hrs.
39	Oct. 17, 1842.	Mary Davis, aged 23, Reading.	Mr. T. B. Hooper, Reading Medical Society, Lancet, 1843, vol. xliii, p. 689.	Mr. Hooper.	A large tumour, arising from the sacrum.	3 days.		D.		D.+	40 hrs.
40	Mar. 8, 1842.	Mary Jepson, aged 43, a weaver, Darwen.	Mr. S. H. Wraith, Darwen, Prov. Med. Jour., vol. v, p. 329, 1842-43.	Mr. Wraith.	Distorted pelvis, from malacosteon.	10 hours.		D.		D.	3 hours.
41	Feb. 22, 1843.	Mary Forrest, aged 38, a weaver, Stockport.	Dr. Radford, Med. Gazette, vol. xlvii, p. 801; Prov. Med. & Sur. Jl., vol. xv, p. 287, 1851.	Dr. Radford.	Distorted pelvis, from malacosteon.	53 hours.		D.		D.	About 27 hrs.
42	July, 1825.	Betty Wilcock, aged nearly 40.	Messrs. Hardy and Bailey, Ass. Med. Jl., vol. iv, p. 48, 1856.	Mr. Bailey.	Distorted pelvis, from mollities ossium.	83 hours.		D.	P.*		61½ hrs.
43	Oct. 18, 1837.	E. M., aged 25, Sunderland.	Mr. J. Ward, Lond. Med. Gazette, vol. xxi, p. 817.	Mr. J. Ward.	Distorted pelvis, from (presumed) rickets	27 to 30 hours.		D.		D.+	5 days 7½ hrs.
44	1840.	..	Dr. Churchill's Operative Midwifery, Table, p. 205, communicated in a letter to Dr. C.	Dr. Elliott, Waterford, Ireland.	Distortion of pelvis; kind not mentioned.			D.		D.	
45	Feb. 1842.	Helen McKenzie, aged 35.	Mr. Alex. Ross, London and Edin. Monthly Journal, vol. ii, p. 425.	Mr. A. Ross, Invergordon.	Distortion of pelvis, most probably mollities ossium (outlet contracted). Tuberosities of ischia approximated very closely; coccyx closing up lower part.	Midwife stated she had been in labour, more or less, for 12 days. Much time elapsed after Mr. Ross decided on necessity of operation.		D.	P.		5 days 7 hrs.
46	August, 1841.	Rebecca Brooks, aged 27, Welford.	Mr. Fred. Cox, Prov. Med. and Surg. Journal, vol. viii, p. 382.	Mr. F. Cox, Welford.	Distortion of pelvis, most likely rickety, but not stated.	30 to 40 hours.		D.		D.‡	
47	Feb. 21, 1845.	Wife of Richard Instan, aged 40.	Mr. J. Milman Coley, Pamphlet.	Mr. Coley.	Distortion of pelvis, said to be rickety.	At least 10 days.		D.		D.	
48	March, 1845.	Mrs. R., Shuttlestone.	Mr. William Lyon, Lon. & Edin. Jour. of Med. Science, vol. v, p. 885.	Mr. Lyon.	A large tumour, the size of a child's head.	72 hours.		D.	P.		
49	Nov. 1845.	Mrs. Sankey, aged 41, Salford.	Dr. Radford, Lond. Med. Gaz., vol. xlvii, p 891; Prov. Med. & Sur. Jl., vol. xv, p. 315, 1851.	Mr. Goodman, assisted by Dr. Radford.	Distortion of pelvis from mollities ossium.	12 to 14 hours.	P.		P.		
50	Jan. 1847.	Sarah Bartlett, aged 37, removed for operation to St. Bartholomew's Hospital London.	Lancet, 1847, vol. i, p. 139.	Mr. Skey, London.	Distortion, from rickets.	5 hrs. 5 min.		D.	P.		36 hrs.

* Two.   + Dead before operation.   ‡ Craniotomy.

TABLE OF CASES OF CÆSAREAN SECTION (continued).

No.	Year	Name and residence of the patient	By whom and where the case is related	Operator	Cause of difficulty	Duration of the labour	Mother Pre-serv'd	Mother Died	Child Pre-serv'd	Child Died	Mother survived
51	June, 1847.	Mrs. Toft, aged 30.	Dr. Radford, Lond. Med. Gazette, vol. xlviii, p. 238; Prov. Med. & Sur. Jl., vol. xv, p. 483, 1851.	Mr. Jas. Braid, Manchester.	Distorted pelvis, from mollities ossium.	3 days, and 10 to 12 hours.		D.		D.*	5½ hrs.
52	1849.	Mrs. Rogers, aged 40, six miles from Lisburn, in a mountainous district.	Mr. Jno. Campbell, Lisburn, Ireland, Lond. Med. Gazette, vol. xliii, p. 1105.	Mr. Campbell.	Distorted pelvis, from mollities ossium. Clearly so, from the account of the case.	52 hours.		D.	P.		7 days.
53	May, 1840.	Mary Haigh, aged 31, near Ashton-under-Lyne.	Dr. Radford. Read at Worcester, at meeting of Prov. Med. Assoc., Aug. 1, 1849. Prov. Med. & Surg. Jl., afterwards in Lond. Med. Gaz., vol. xlvii, p. 1110.	Mr. Cluley, assisted by Dr. Radford.	Distorted pelvis, from mollities ossium.	Slight pains for two or three days. Membranes unruptured until a few hours before operation.	P.		P.		
54	May, 1850.	Elizabeth Williams, in the 27th year of her age.	Dr. Chas. West, Med.-Chir. Trans., vol. xxxiv, p. 61.	Mr. Skey.	Distorted pelvis, from mollities ossium.	16 hours.		D.	P.		108½ hrs.
55	May, 1850.	Mrs. Kennaway, aged 43.	Mr. M. Nimmo, Dundee, Mon. Jour. Med. Science, Sept. 1850, p. 226.	Mr. Nimmo.	Distorted pelvis, from mollities ossium.	5 days. Occasional pains; but had regular labour for 17½ hours.		D.	P.		Scarcely 3 hrs.
56	Sept. 1850.	Sarah —, Bethnal Green, aged 23.	Dr. Henry Oldham, London, Med.-Chir. Trans., vol. xxxiv, p. 89.	Mr. Poland, London.	Distortion of the pelvis from rickets.	84 hours from the time labour was artificially induced.		D.		D.+	About 44 hrs.
57	June, 1851.	Sarah L., aged 28.	Dr. Henry Oldham, Guy's Hosp. Reports, vol. vii, p. 426.	Mr. Poland.	Cancer of the cervix uteri.	Indefinite slight uterine contractions for 2 or 3 days. Membranes ruptured about 12 hours before operation.	P.		P.		Recovered from.
58	Nov. 1851.	Ann Kenyon, aged 31.	Dr. Broughton, manuscript.	Dr. Broughton, Preston, assisted by Dr. Radford and Dr. Whitehead.	Distorted pelvis, from mollities ossium.	11 hours.		D.	P.		5 days 2 hrs.
59	1853.	Aged 41.	Dr. Charles Waller, Medical Times and Gazette, vol. vi, p. 266.	Mr. Le Gros Clark.	Large fibrous tumour.	30 hours. Membranes ruptured 78 hours before operation.		D.	P.		36 hrs.
60	Feb. 28, 1848.	Mrs. Y., Shaftesbury, Dorset, aged 42.	Mr. R. W. Sanneman, Chelsea, Lancet, vol. ii, 1850, p. 50.	Mr. Sanneman.	Distortion of the pelvis, from mollities ossium.	12 hours.		D.		D.	23 hrs.
61	June 24, 1854.	Mrs. —, Cupar, Scotland.	Professor Simpson, Edinburgh, Assoc. Med. Jour., vol. ii, 1854, p. 1066.	Professor Simpson.	Distortion of the pelvis, from mollities ossium.	60 or 70 hours.		D.		D.‡	
62	1854.	Mary A. Johnson, aged 31.	Paper read at Royal Med. & Chir. Soc., April 13, 1858; from notes kindly furnished by Dr. Greenhalgh to me.	Dr. Greenhalgh.	Distortion of the pelvis, from mollities ossium.	About 6 hours.		D.	P.		3 weeks.
63	1854.	Lydia Lowdey.	Notes kindly furnished me by Dr. Greenhalgh.	Dr. Greenhalgh.	Distortion of the pelvis, from rickets.	12 hours.		D.	P.		4 days.
64	Dec. 5, 1854.	Martha C., Nottingham.	Dr. J. C. L. Marsh, Lancet, vol. ii, 1863, p. 500.	Dr. Marsh.	Distortion of the pelvis, from mollities ossium.	55½ hours.		D.	P.		48 hrs.
65	Feb. 29, 1856.	Mrs. Runham, Lawton, aged 30.	Mr. Humphry, Assoc. Med. Jour., vol. iv, 1856, p. 779.	Mr. Humphry.	Distortion of the pelvis, from mollities ossium.	Not definitely stated; but most likely about 30 hours.		D.		D.§	20 hrs.
66	Feb. 25, 1856.	Nancy Nixon, aged 27, a travelling hawker, in a miserably low cellar, Staleybridge, Lancash.	Dr. Chas. Clay, Midland Quarterly Journal of the Medical Sciences, part i, p. 21.	Dr. Clay.	A large tumour of a firm fibro-cartilaginous texture.	3 days.		D.		D.‖	19 days.
67	Oct. 1, 1856.	Anne N.	Dr. W. H. Thornton, Lancet, vol. i, 1857, p. 313.	Dr. Thornton.	A bony projection from promontory of sacrum, evidently exostosis; perhaps cellulated.	About 18 hours.	P.			D.*	
68	Feb. 19, 1858.	Matilda T., aged 20, Newport, Monmouthshire.	Mr. Jas. Hawkins, Lancet, vol. i, 1858, p. 529.	Mr. Hawkins.	Distortion of pelvis; kind of deformity not stated; but as lameness and inability to walk in early life, it was most probably from rickets.	Not definitely stated.	P.		P.		Lived.

* Dead before operation.   + Head perforated.   ‡ Living; died soon after.
§ Embryotomy had begun; the arm removed.   ‖ Alive when extracted; but died in a few seconds.

TABLE OF CASES OF CÆSAREAN SECTION (concluded).

No.	Year.	Name and residence of the patient.	By whom and where the case is related.	Operator.	Cause of difficulty.	Duration of the labour.	Mother.		Child.		Mother survived.
							Pre-serv'd	Died	Pre-serv'd	Died	
69	July 12, 1858.	Mrs. N., aged 30, Harrington; brought to University College Hospital.	Dr. Murphy, Dub. Quar. Jour. of Med. Sc., vol. xxvii, (new series), p. 108.	Mr. Quain.	Distortion of the pelvis, from mollities ossium.	As far as can be computed, 4 days.		D.		D.	Nearly 48 hrs.
70	Dec. 1859.	Mrs. H., Walton-le-dale, near Preston, Lancashire.	Dr. H. Ashton, Lancet, vol. i, 1860, p. 440.	Dr. Ashton.	Distortion of the pelvis, from mollities osseum.	As far as can be ascertained from the data, about 17 or 18 hours.		D.	P.		25 hrs.
71	Dec. 10, 1860.	Emma P.	Dr. Jas. Edmunds, Lancet, vol. i, 1861, p. 4.	Dr. Edmunds.	Hard cancer of os and cervix uteri.	Fully 6 days.	P.		P.		Lived.
72	Feb. 2, 1861.	Isabella King, unmarried, aged 23, Aberdeen, Scotland.	Dr. Robert Dyce, Edin. Med. Jour., vol. vii, p. 895.	Dr. Dyce.	Distortion of the pelvis, from rickets.	As far as can be computed, 4 to 5 days.		D.		D.*	43 hrs.
73	Aug. 7, 1862.	E. M., unmarried, aged 17, Tottenhall.	Dr. David Johnson, Lancet, vol. ii, 1862, p. 475.	Dr. Johnson.	Small underdeveloped pelvis, perhaps rickety. Antero-posterior diameter only, ascertained per vaginam to be 2¼ in. Preternatural position of child, right hand and the two feet.	12 hours, when first seen by Dr. J.; afterwards the time in his attempt to deliver, etc., 17 hrs.		D.		D.†	46 hrs.
74	Dec. 24, 1862.	Mary Ann —, unmarried, aged 42, Kingswood, Bristol.	Dr. J. G. Swayne, Obstetric Trans., vol. v, 1863, p. 84.	Mr. Coe, at the Bristol General Hospital.	Distortion of the pelvis, from congenital malformation. It was like that produced by rickets.	60 hours befor she came to the hospital, and a few hours after her arrival.		D.	P.		42 hrs.
75	1863.	Eliza Hubbard, St. Bartholomew's Hospital.	Dr. Greenhalgh, private communication.	Mr. Skey.	Medullary tumour.	18 hours.		D.		D.	18 hrs.
76	Sep. 10, 1864.	Mary Salimson, City of London Lying-in Hospital, aged 26.	Dr. Greenhalgh, private communication.	Dr. Greenhalgh.	Distortion of the pelvis, from rickets.	About 41 hours.		D.	P.		48½ hrs.
77	Nov. 23, 1864.	Ann Burgess, No. 1, Brown Street, Acton Street, London Road, Manchester.	Dr. Thomas Pigg.	Dr. Clay.	Malacosteon.	Strong pains for 24 hours, but had probably been in labour to some extent before this.		D.	P.		3 days.

* Turning ineffectually attempted. Craniotomy was also unsuccessfully performed.   † Dead before operation.

APPENDIX.

DURING the time the foregoing observations were passing through the press, I determined to reprint the seven cases of Cæsarean section which had been previously published. I have preferred giving them as they originally appeared, rather than making any abbreviations of them, although many remarks which are appended to them will be found to have been already made in the preceding observations, etc. I have affixed to each case the number under which it is registered in the table. One case is now published for the first time.

I have given outline sketches of the brims of most of the pelves belonging to the women whose cases are hereafter related. Those measurements which were obtained after death (with the exception of that belonging to Mary Haigh) were made after all the soft parts had been removed, so that they (the measurements) are really greater than they would have been found, with the addition of the pelvic organs and tissues.

I have given two delineations of each of the pelves of the cases Nos. (Tab.) 49 and 53. One shows as accurately as possible the state of the pelvis when the operation was performed ; the other indicates the degree of diminution which had taken place after this time up to the death of each of the patients. The cavities and outlets of all the pelves were relatively quite as much diminished as the brims are represented to have been.

CASE (Tab.) 27 (*Unsuccessful*). On Sunday, the 1st of April, 1820, I was requested to visit Mary Ashworth, residing at Denton, about six miles from Manchester. I was told she was in great danger, having been in labour a considerable length of time, and that no progress was made in the case. This report did not surprise me when I ascertained who the individual was ; for Mr. Wood, my partner and esteemed relative, had visited her about the end of the seventh month of her present pregnancy, at the request of her medical attendant, Mr. Morris, a highly respectable surgeon, who resided at Ashton-under-Lyne. Mr. Wood at this period examined her *per vaginam*, and his opinion was, that if her pregnancy did proceed, when labour came on, the Cæsarean section would be required, as in her case no other means would be of the least avail. At three o'clock, p.m., I reached her dwelling, and found Mr. Morris and Mr. Cheetham awaiting my arrival.

I was informed by Mr. Morris that she had been in strong labour about thirty-four hours ; that the membranes had ruptured in two hours after its commencement, and that the *liquor amnii* had gradually passed away. He had not been able to feel the presentation nor the *os uteri*. The pains were strong for twenty-fours, but after-

a

wards gradually abated. The urine had been passed freely during the Saturday, but this day (Sunday) there was no evidence of any having been discharged. The bowels were constipated, and had not been opened during the labour.

Her previous history was to the following effect :—She had borne ten children, nine of whom were expelled by the natural powers. In the last labour, considerable difficulty occurred, and the practitioner had recourse to craniotomy. During her tenth pregnancy, she experienced considerable weakness in her loins, and felt rheumatic pains about the hips, and limped in her gait. These pains continued from that time till her present pregnancy, but did not increase in degree. When she again became pregnant, her sufferings increased, and her lameness became more manifest. Her stature was now observed to diminish in height. She was 42 years of age, and was employed as a hat-trimmer.

I found her in bed, lying upon the back, with the head and shoulders raised. She moved with the greatest difficulty. The pulse was feeble and frequent, beating about 150 in the minute. She had often vomited, and had great tenderness in the belly, which was considerably increased by pressure. Her tongue was furred and dry, and she complained of great thirst ; her countenance expressed considerable anguish. Being requested to compose her mind, she answered, " she was composed, but anxious for relief, and would suffer any pain so that she might be delivered."

Upon examining the abdomen, I found the uterus projecting very much forwards, and lying with its anterior surface upon the upper part of the thighs. By a vaginal examination, I discovered that the labia were much swelled, and the vagina felt dry and rough ; it was hotter than natural, and an odour similar to that arising from animal matter when partially decomposed was perceived from the hand when it was withdrawn. The outlet of the pelvis had undergone great change ; the arch of the pubes was totally destroyed by the near approximation of the rami of the ischia and pubes, having only a small slit, so narrow at the upper and lower parts as not to admit the point of the index finger ; at the middle, however, the finger could just be introduced. The tuberosities of the ischia were not more than one inch and a half to one inch and three quarters as under ; and the lower portion of the sacrum was so much more incurvated than natural, as to throw the coccyx much more forward, and consequently lessen the conjugate diameter of the lower aperture of the pelvis. This great diminution in the outlet rendered it difficult to pass the hand in order to measure the brim, and it was found necessary to carry it very far backward in order to accomplish it. This aperture was found much more altered than the outlet ; one finger only edgeways could be placed between the points of bone in the conjugate diameter. In traversing it from side to side, I could detect no great difference, but if there was any, the left was the most contracted. In the transverse diameter, I could just place three fingers parallel to each other. The figure* of the brim was tripartite, having a slit on each side, and a third passing forwards, produced by the approximation and jutting out of the pubes, which was so narrow that the finger could not pass within it. This alteration in the brim was occasioned by the falling downwards and forwards of the upper part of the sacrum, and the

---

* See Figure 1st.

lower lumbar vertebra, and by the body of the *ossa pubis* and ischii being forced backwards and inwards, whilst the symphyses and rami of the pubes projected forwards and upwards. The measurement of the conjugate diameter did not exceed three-quarters of an inch, or that of the transverse two inches; and having placed my fingers upon each other in the widest part, and having measured them when withdrawn, I concluded that no body of a diameter greater than from three-quarters to an inch could pass through it; and that delivery *per vias naturales*, aided by the crotchet, was utterly impracticable. Another important feature in the case was, that no part of the child or *os uteri* could be felt.

Upon these grounds, then, we concluded that our only resource was the Cæsarean section. Our opinions were now stated to the husband and friends, and they cheerfully submitted to any practice we thought best to adopt. The patient, anxious to have her sufferings ter-minated, also readily acquiesced in our decision.

An enema was ordered to be administered, and it soon operated. The catheter was also introduced, but little urine was withdrawn. As the patient felt cold, a little warm wine and water was given, which acted beneficially. Having placed her upon a table, an incision of six inches long was made through the abdominal integuments, about one inch to the left of the umbilicus, extending from three inches above to three below. A small opening was made into the peritoneum, and this membrane was afterwards fully divided by a probe-pointed bistoury. The uterus was now exposed, and an excision of equal length was made into this organ, nearly dividing its entire substance. An opening was now made at the lowest point of the wound by the knife, so as to admit the finger, upon which the bistoury was again passed, and the uterus was laid open. I now passed my hand, and, taking hold of the thigh of the child, readily extracted it; but, unfortunately, it was dead. The funis having been divided, the placental portion was held firmly in the left hand, whilst the right was introduced into the uterus to extract the placenta, which was attached to the upper and posterior part of the uterus. As soon as the placenta was removed, the uterus energetically contracted, and lowering itself became almost invisible. The intestines protruded at the wound, but were soon reduced and retained by the hands extended over their surface. Mr. Morris next passed several ligatures through the abdominal parietes, and afterwards applied slips of adhesive plaster, by which the edges of the wound were closely approximated. Pledgets of lint, spread with cerate, were also applied, and in order to secure the whole, a broad bandage was loosely put on. The quantity of blood lost was trivial, not exceeding three or four ounces, which favourable circumstance, doubtless, was partly owing to the position of the placenta, and partly to the vigorous contraction of the uterus.

During the whole course of the operation the patient maintained the greatest fortitude, and expressed her thankfulness upon the termination of her sufferings. She, however, as well as all present, was disappointed that the child was lost.

The patient was then put to bed, and, as the pulse was rather low, a cordial was administered, which in a little while revived her. An anodyne draught, containing sixty minims of laudanum, was also given.

At ten o'clock P.M. the pulse was 140; the skin was hot; she was thirsty, and complained of headache; belly tender; discharge not more than usual; thinks she can sleep; no urine passed.

April 2nd, eight o'clock A.M. Says she has slept; has taken some refreshment; skin hotter; pulse 140 to 150 in the minute, and feels sharp to the finger; has not voided any urine; bowels not moved. Ordered saline effervescing draughts. The catheter to be introduced, by which from three to four ounces of urine were withdrawn.

Twelve o'clock, noon. Not so well; had shivering and some vomiting; the pulse was more frequent, and the abdominal tenderness increased; belly swelled; a sanious discharge was oozing from the wound; bandage uncomfortable; vaginal discharge rather greater and more offensive; bowels not moved. The medicines were continued, and the bandage loosened.

Four o'clock P.M. Has again shivered; continues to vomit; pulse more frequent and tremulous; countenance more depressed; abdomen more tender and more swelled; is very thirsty, and her tongue is very much loaded; the bowels still constipated. The saline medicines were continued, and an enema with oil of turpentine and castor oil was ordered to be administered.

Ten o'clock P.M. Vomiting continues unabated; pulse still very frequent and much weaker; skin colder and rather clammy; is slightly incoherent; belly very tender and much swelled; discharge offensive; has not passed urine; the enema operated. The catheter introduced, and four ounces of urine withdrawn; the bandage still further loosened; to have a little brandy in her gruel; to take forty minims of laudanum. The symptoms continued to grow more unfavourable during the night, and she died at four o'clock this morning (Tuesday) about thirty-five hours after the operation.

An application was made to examine the body, but permission was only granted under a promise that the wound was alone to be inspected; but Mr. Morris, while alone, took the opportunity of ascertaining, as far as he was able, the state of the parts. The edges of the external wound were quite separate, and had a flabby unhealthy aspect. Having divided the stitches, and drawn aside the integuments, the uterus was observed to be well contracted. The wound was much diminished, its edges were loose and unhealthy. The peritoneum was inflamed, and about from four to six ounces of serum were effused within its cavity. Upon again raising the uterus, the cervix was seen to be dark-coloured, and having divided it, the lower portion and orifice were found in a gangrenous state. The bladder was empty, and uninjured. The brim of the pelvis was examined, and found fully as much distorted as I have before mentioned.

REMARKS. The issue of this case presents indisputable evidence of the serious mischief arising from protracting the operation. Both the life of the mother and the child were most likely forfeited by the delay. How the real character of the case could have been so much overlooked, after the clear and decided opinion of Mr. Wood, given at the end of the seventh month, I am at a loss to conceive.

The tumefaction of the external genitals, and the inflamed condition of the vagina, are alone to be attributed to the too frequent examinations made. When a practitioner undertakes to explore for the exact measurements of the brim of the pelvis, deformed like the one belonging to the subject of this case, he is compelled to pass his hand completely into the vagina, and, from an anxiety to accomplish this, and to ascertain the nature of the presentation of the child, he is induced to repeat the operation very often. These repeated examinations are often productive of very serious mischief, causing inflammation, which frequently terminates in suppuration and sloughing. With these circumstances before us, we are of opinion that every unnecessary manœuvre ought to be avoided, and that the practitioner should acquaint himself, as completely as it is possible, with the nature of the case, before he withdraws his hand.

Case (Tab.) 30 (*Unsuccessful*). Mary Nixon, aged 39, had been married sixteen years, and had been pregnant eight times, in seven of which she reached the full period of gestation, and in one she miscarried once at the fourth month, which happened about thirteen months before her present pregnancy. The last natural labour took place about four years since, and was so rapid as to be completed in two or three hours. She had enjoyed good health until about two years ago, when she began to suffer from what she called rheumatism and a short cough. Afterwards she was frequently confined to bed, and her friends observed her to rather diminish in height. The pains in her back and hips increased in violence during her present pregnancy, and her height is now very considerably diminished. She has been employed as an "ender and mender" for the manufacturers, which occupation has obliged her to be sedentary, but has attended to her domestic duties, although unfit.

At one o'clock on Thursday morning, May 24th, 1821, she was apprised of the approach of labour by a discharge of water, which continued to dribble away without pain. At four o'clock, Mrs. Barber, her midwife, was sent for, as she now felt slight pains. On examination *per vaginam* Mrs. B. could neither feel the *os uteri* nor any part of the child, but ascertained that the pelvis was considerably distorted. At noon she sent for Mr. Wilson, one of the surgeons of the Manchester Lying-in Hospital, but he was from home, and instead of immediately applying elsewhere, she allowed several hours to elapse before she sent for other assistance. At eight o'clock P.M., Mr. K. Wood saw the patient, and considered the case of such importance as to induce him to call upon Mr. Wilson, who was then at home, and they immediately went to the house, and reached it at a quarter before nine o'clock. Mr. Wilson agreed in his opinion, and he desired that a general consultation of the medical officers of the institution might be immediately called.

At ten o'clock P.M., when Dr. Hull, Mr. Wilson, Mr. K. Wood, Mr. Lowe, and Dr. Radford had assembled, the state of the patient was as follows:—Her pulse was 130; the skin hotter than natural; her tongue was furred; she was very thirsty; her countenance was cheerful; she had passed urine at several intervals during her labour, and her bowels had responded three times to an enema which her midwife had very judiciously administered. The stools were scanty, and of a green colour. The pains, which were reported to have been very frequent during the afternoon, continued so. She complained of great tenderness in the belly, which was considerably increased by pressure. The distance between the pubes and sternum was much shorter than natural. The *fundus uteri* projected very much forwards, and had an inclination to the left side. By an examination *per vaginam*, I found the parts soft, moist, and cool. The sacrum was considerably more incurvated than natural, and the coccyx projected upwards into the cavity of the pelvis. The tuberosities of the ischia approached very near together at the fore-part, and the rami of the ischia and pubes approximated so closely together as not to admit a finger to pass between them along any part, except at the middle, at which place there was a small opening, in consequence of a slight bulging outwards of the bone on either side. The pubic arch was destroyed, and only a small chink left, by which the depth of the pelvis was increased at the anterior part. In order to examine the brim I passed my hand, but was compelled to carry it very much backwards. The pubes on each side formed a very acute angle at their fore part, and then running forwards nearly parallel to the symphysis, having a slit between them which would barely admit the finger edgeways. The base of the sacrum and the last lumbar vertebræ had sunk forwards and downwards into the pelvis, and diminished the conjugate diameter on the left side so much as barely to admit the finger in the position, that when it was withdrawn, it measured three-quarters of an inch, and when placed in other parts of the brim, an inch, as far as could be ascertained, was the fullest latitude which could be given to guide us in our decision.* We all agreed that no other means but the Cæsarean section could avail us to deliver this poor creature.

Having decided upon our plan, we stated our opinions to the friends, who readily consented that we should adopt any practice we thought best. When we acquainted the patient with the difficulty of her case, and the operation necessary to extricate the child, she unhesitatingly acquiesed. It was intended to have used the catheter, but this was unnecessary, as half a pint of urine was discharged by her own efforts.

She was now placed upon a table, and a little brandy and water, with thirty drops of laudanum, was administered her.

Mr. Wilson made a longitudinal incision a little to the left of the umbilicus, six inches in length, extending from three inches above to three inches below this part, and divided the abdominal parietes down to the peritoneum. A small opening was made through this membrane, and it was fully divided by a probe-pointed bistoury, passed along with the finger. An incision was now made nearly through the uterus, corresponding in length and direction to the external wound. The probe-pointed bistoury was introduced on the finger through a small opening, and the remaining portion divided. This exposed the child, which lay with its breech towards the opening. Mr. K. Wood seized the child by one thigh, and the body was extracted with the greatest ease, until the shoulders came to pass, when the uterus suddenly and powerfully contracted, and grasped the child's neck and left arm so strongly that this gentleman could not liberate it, although he used great force in extraction. He then gradually passed his hand along the body of the child into the uterus, and having dilated the structure the child was extracted. It would have been easier to have torn away the uterus from its connections than to have brought the child away by direct extractive force. The fundus and body of the uterus felt very hard. The child was vigorously alive when first taken hold of, but from the length of time occupied in extracting the head, it became so enfeebled as to show only slight signs of life. I very diligently employed every means to resuscitate it, and continued them for at least three-

---

* See Figure 2nd.

quarters of an hour, but was ultimately unsuccessful. This was a most appalling affair. After dividing the funis, the placental extremity was firmly held with one hand, whilst the other was introduced into the cavity of the uterus, for the purpose of removing the placenta, which was already detached, and lying loose. The uterus then immediately fully contracted.

The intestines, which appeared at the wound, were replaced and retained by the extended hand ; the edges of the wound were then brought together by ligatures, supported by strips of adhesive plaster and an extended bandage.

Very little blood was lost during the operation, a small branch of the epigastric only being divided. Its bleeding was restrained by the pressure of the finger.

The patient felt faint whilst on the table, but was soon recruited by taking a little brandy and water, When all was adjusted she was carried to bed, and said she was quite as comfortable as she could possibly expect. The pulse now beat about 136 in the minute, and was distinct. The heat of the skin was not much above natural. In half an hour afterwards she felt a distressing sensation at the chest ; her heart beat very quickly, and the breathing became very much hurried ; her skin grew cold, and the vaginal discharge was increased, but still not in such a quantity as to create alarm. Thirty drops of laudanum in a little brandy and water were immediately administered, and in half an hour forty drops more. In a very short time all these symptoms subsided, and she felt as well and as warm as before. All stimulants were now prohibited, and the antiphlogistic regimen recommended, and she was left for the night in the charge of Mr. Hunt, at that time a pupil of Mr. Wilson's.

Friday, May 25th, seven o'clock, A.M. Present, Dr. Hull, Mr. Wilson, Mr. K. Wood, and Dr. Radford. She experienced no further palpitation of the heart ; slept tolerably well ; the pulse was 131 ; respiration easy ; skin rather hot ; belly feels comfortable and not swelled. To take a saline effervescent draught every three hours, and an ounce of the almond mixture with five drops of laudanum in the intervals.

Twelve o'clock, noon. Present, Mr. Wilson, Mr. Hudson, Mr. K. Wood, and Dr. Radford. The heart appeared to jerk ; pulse 130, and quite distinct ; skin hotter ; her countenance more anxious ; tongue furred, but moist ; has again slept ; urine passed twice. The medicines were continued.

Four o'clock, P.M. Present, Mr. Wood, Mr. Wilson, Mr. K. Wood, and Dr. Radford. Belly rather tense ; pulse 130, and firmer ; tongue dry and furred ; is thirsty ; has passed urine ; her cough is still troublesome ; the bowels are constipated. A solution of Epsom salts in infusion of roses was directed to be given until it operated, and a linctus for the cough was ordered.

Six o'clock, P.M. Present, Dr. Hull, Mr. Wilson, and Dr. Radford. Her countenance looked better ; the heart throbbed violently ; her pulse beat 125 ; the tongue was rather more moist and soft ; the belly continued very tense ; and the respiration was hurried ; she has had slight vomiting, and her bowels have not yet been moved. The medicines were continued.

Ten o'clock, P.M. Present, Mr. Wilson, Mr. Lowe, and Dr. Radford. Her countenance has become more anxious ; her respiration is more laborious, and she has again vomited. The skin is hotter ; her belly is very tender, and is much swelled ; her pulse is 130 ; the vaginal discharge trifling, and very slightly coloured ; she has a tendency to doze ; has had several fœtid liquid stools.

To omit the aperient, but to continue the other medicine ; the bandage to be loosened.

26th, Saturday, eight o'clock, A.M. Present, Mr. Wood, Mr. Wilson, Mr. K. Wood, and Dr. Radford. Has frequently vomited a brown slimy fluid ; her pulse is 130; her respiration still laborious ; the belly rather softer; her skin is still hot; and the lochial discharge very trifling.

Ten o'clock, A.M. Present, Dr. Hull, Mr. Wilson, and Dr. Radford. Pulse 134; vomiting has ceased.

One o'clock, P.M. Present, Mr. Wood, Mr. Wilson, and Dr. Radford. Her hands feel cold ; the pulse is 130; her mind is clear; the vomiting has ceased; lochial discharge fœtid and more profuse; and there has been a thin and offensive sanious discharge from the wound.

Five o'clock, P.M. Symptoms still grow worse.

Ten o'clock, P.M. Present, Mr. Wood, Mr. K. Wood, and Dr. Radford. The symptoms continue to become more unfavourable.

Sunday, eight o'clock, A.M. Pulse 140, and very weak; the skin is rather cold, and covered with a slight clammy sweat; her countenance is very anxious; and there is great swelling and tenderness of the belly; the lochial discharge is very offensive ; she has not passed urine. The lowest strap of adhesive plaster being removed, the wound appeared in an unhealthy state and not united; a great discharge took place, which was very offensive. During this day (Sunday) she was visited several times, and found still further sinking. At six o'clock in the evening she expired, having lived sixty-seven hours and a half after the operation.

REMARKS. It may appear strange that no notice was taken of this poor woman's case at an earlier period of pregnancy, as she was a patient of the Lying-in Hospital. But our hospital extends its aid only to poor women at their own houses; and this poor creature having obtained a note of recommendation from a subscriber, was admitted, the medical officers having no knowledge that such a case was on the books. Another unfortunate circumstance was the midwife omitting to send for other surgical assistance in the absence of Mr. Wilson, thereby allowing several valuable hours to elapse.

The violent contraction of the uterus, by which the head and left arm of the child were seized after the extraction of the trunk and lower extremities, forms a remarkable feature in the case. The placenta was found detached and lying loose in the cavity of the uterus ; and how far this violent contraction depended upon this circumstance is difficult to say. In natural labour we well know that as soon as the placenta is detached, the energies of the fundus and body of the uterus are aroused, and contraction follows, and is continued until this mass is expelled. In the former case of Cæsarean operation the uterus was quiescent, until the placenta was detached by the hand, when contraction instantaneously followed.

CASE (Tab.) 41* (*Unsuccessful*). On Tuesday evening, February 21st,

---

* This (No. 41) case is reprinted from the *Provincial Medical and Surgical Journal*, vol. xv, p. 18. It was also originally published in the *London Medical Gazette*, vol. xlvii, p. 801, 1851, in which a great mistake has been made by the printers, in misplacing some of the first sheets of the manuscript, and which has created great confusion in the meaning. I have adverted to this error in order that it may be, when possible, in some measure corrected.

1841, Mr. Dunn, Surgeon of Manchester, and Mr. Goulden, of Stockport, called upon me to request my opinion on the case of Mary Forrest, who resided at Stockport. She was the patient of the latter named gentleman, from whom I learnt the following particulars :— He had visited her at one o'clock P.M. (on Monday) the day before. She was at the full period of gestation, and had violent and regular pains in the back. Mr. Goulden made a vaginal examination, and found the pelvis very much distorted : he thought she could not be delivered unless by the Cæsarean section. A grain of opium was ordered to be taken every two or three hours until the pains abated, which happened after six doses had been taken. When Mr. G. visited her on Tuesday morning, he found her nearly free from pain. Her bowels being constipated, some pills composed of aloes and calomel were prescribed. He again examined her *per vaginam*, and concluded that her delivery was impossible, except by the means already stated. He further said on the evening of this day (Tuesday), when at my house, that she was now entirely free from pain, and, on inquiry, said he did not think labour had commenced. The object of his coming over to Manchester was to request me to visit the patient the following day and examine the pelvis; so that clear and definite views might be had, and what course should be adopted when labour came on. On Wednesday, I accompanied Mr. Dunn to Stockport. We found Mary Forrest in bed, and so helpless as to be unable to turn herself. Her countenance was short and inexpressive ; her lips thick ; her eyes blue; on the corner of the right eye there was a considerable opacity, the result of an injury from having been struck by a shuttle. She had been employed as a power-loom weaver in a cotton factory. Her age was thirty-eight years. Her first labour, which was natural, happened nineteen years since, and the child was a boy. About eighteen months before her present labour she became pregnant a second time, and aborted at the end of two months. She had suffered during the last five or six years violent rheumatic pains, but otherwise her health had been good until within the last few months. Her stature had become considerably less, and her legs and thighs were very œdematous. She said she felt the movements of the infant, which, on first placing my hand on the abdomen, I thought I perceived; but, keeping it steadily applied, I soon found it was only slight contraction of the uterus. The stethoscope was used, but gave no evidence of its being alive. The abdominal parietes were very thin and felt very flabby. The uterus projected very much forward, and lay over the symphysis pubis to such a degree, that when the patient was placed in a sitting posture in the bed its anterior surface rested on her thighs. Her breech was gibbous, and her thighs approximated considerably more than natural. The discharge from the vagina was of a dark colour, and had a putrid smell.

Her constitutional condition was very bad. Pulse 140 ; tongue furred ; great thirst ; continued vomiting ; great abdominal tenderness and tension; bowels not moved for two days. By a vaginal examination the pelvis was found to be considerably distorted. The outlet was so much diminished as to render it difficult to pass the hand, in order to ascertain as precisely as possible the measurement of its several parts. The arch of the pubes was nearly destroyed by the near approximation of the rami of the ischia and pubes, there being only a narrow slit, which just admitted the point of the finger. Between the tuberosities of the ischia I could barely place three fingers. The coccyx was considerably incurvated upwards and forwards. The brim was tripartite in figure, or composed of three divisions. This altered shape was produced by the upper portion of the sacrum, and the last lumbar vertebræ standing so very much forwards and downwards, inclining a little more to the right side; and by the body of the ossa pubis and ischii being forced backwards and inwards, and the rami and symphysis pubis jutting forwards. On the right side I could just place the point of the index finger, and on the left I could pass two fingers, one lying partially over the other.* Neither the presentation of the child nor the *os uteri* could be felt.

Although my attendance was specially requested to explore the pelvis in anticipation of labour, and conclude on the measures which must be adopted when it supervened, we were compelled now to decide on her delivery, as she was and had been in labour since Monday, when the membranes must have ruptured, as I ascertained she had a dribbling watery discharge afterwards. We unanimously agreed that she could only be delivered by the Cæsarean section. When we apprised this poor creature of our decision, she readily consented to submit to any plan we considered necessary. An enema was administered, but it did not act. The catheter was passed and about an ounce of urine withdrawn. Afterwards I placed the hand on the abdomen, and found still a fluctuant tumour, which induced me to pass a longer catheter, and, by a careful manipulation, it was carried higher, and succeeded in further removing a considerable quantity of urine.

In the first place, we arranged the duty which each gentleman had to perform. Mr. Cheetham and Mr. Pigott joined us to witness the operation. I commenced to make the incision a little above the umbilicus, on the left side of the linea alba, and extended it downwards towards the pubes, so as to be about six inches in length. In consequence of the very attenuated state of the abdominal parietes the uterus was at once exposed, and its tissues partially cut. It was necessary to raise the defected uterus upwards before the external incision was made. About a pint of water, with a large portion of intestines, now escaped. This portion of bowel, which had been dangerously exposed to be wounded, being drawn aside by Mr. Dunn, I fully divided the uterus in the line of the wound first made into it. The placenta was now exposed, the greater part of which lay to the right side of the incision and maintained its adherence; whilst that on the left (the smaller division) was separated by the contraction of the uterus. Mr. Dunn immediately passed his right hand in search of the feet of the infant, and his left along the body to guard its neck from being spasmodically seized during its abstraction (a caution given to him by me, having, in a previous case, met with this disaster). Having gained a firm hold of the feet of the infant, he very cautiously and expeditiously drew the body forth until the neck came to pass, which was then firmly grasped by the uterus, and the head thereby detained. The womb had an appearance as if it was indented, and strongly reminded us of its condition in hour-glass contraction. The difficulty at last being overcome, the infant (dead and partially putrid) was completely removed. The adherent portion of the placenta was detached, and wholly extracted. Not more than a few ounces of blood were lost. The intestines were much dis-

---

* See Figure 3rd.

tended with air, and were difficult to keep in position during the
operation; and could not be replaced or retained after it, until the
wound was contracted with sutures. Their peritoneal coat was highly
inflamed. The edges of the wound were brought together by interrupted sutures, and maintained by strips of adhesive plaister, and
supported by a bandage placed round the patient. She bore the
operation with great fortitude, and, indeed, scarcely made a complaint during its performance. Afterwards, she said she had not
suffered so much pain as she had felt from some of the unavailing
parturient pains. She now expressed herself as being very comfortable.

Nine o'clock P.M. Considerably worse; pulse 140; tongue furred;
great thirst; vomits continually; surface cool; countenance anxious;
great tenderness of the belly; clyster not returned; had no sleep; a
little urine passed. Ordered to take morph. acet. gr. j.

Thursday, 23rd, two o'clock A.M. Mr. Goulden visited her. Pulse
160; vomiting unabated; matter rejected of a dark colour; skin
rather warm; breathing quick; belly very tender; had no sleep;
bowels still constipated. Ordered morph. acet. gr. j.

Nine o'clock A.M. Mr. Goulden and Mr. Cheetham reported that
she continued to vomit the same fluid; skin warmer; pulse less frequent, and countenance less anxious; bowels moved; passed urine;
lochial discharge; abdomen tense and sore. To take morph. acet.
gr. j., and saline effervescing mixture.

Half-past one o'clock P.M. Mr. Goulden was urgently summoned:
it was stated that she was dying. He found her very drowsy or
lethargic; had great difficulty to rouse her. Pulse 140; countenance more flushed, and rather bluish in colour; no vomiting;
abdomen distended.

Two o'clock P.M. Present, Dr. Radford, Mr. Goulden, Mr. Dunn,
and Mr. Pigott. She still continues very drowsy; pulse 140, and
very tremulous; skin bedewed with cold perspiration; her countenance is sunken, and her cheeks are of a purplish colour; her
breathing very hurried, with mucous *râle*; does not vomit; belly
tympanitic; bowels not moved. Ordered an enema with spt. terebinth., etc.

The symptoms continued to grow worse until seven o'clock (*vespere*), when she expired: having lived about twenty-seven hours
after the operation. Body examined twenty hours after death by
Mr. Dunn and Mr. Gaskell, in the presence of Dr. Radford, Mr.
Goulden, Mr. Pigott, and Mr. H. Winterbottom. General tumefaction
of the abdomen, its parietes being extremely thin. The edges of the
external wound were nearly altogether adherent; adhesion of the
peritoneal surfaces of the intestines and that of the abdominal
parietes. On breaking through these adhesions, about a pint of bloody
serum was discharged. The convolutions of the bowels were firmly
united, and effused lymph was seen on their surfaces. The colon adhered to the uterus.

We were particularly struck by the very remarkable pallidity of
the tissue of the intestines, when compared with their highly injected vascular state seen during the operation. The uterus stood
obliquely; the wound in this organ was three and a half inches long;
its edges were flabby and gaping; the os was very patulous, and its
lips ragged and gangrenous. The lower portion of the cervix was
very soft and dark coloured. The internal surface of the uterus was

softer and darker in colour than usual. The gall bladder large and full; spleen healthy. The left kidney externally natural; its pelvis larger; and it contained a creamy fluid. Right kidney smaller than usual, and contained a similar fluid. The legs very œdematous. Pelvis removed; brim tripartite in shape; found an excessive quantity of fat about the pelvis and back.

From upper edge of the fifth lumbar vertebra to the inner surface of the symphysis pubis two inches and six-eighths.

From side of the said vertebra to the ilium behind the acetabulum on the left side, five-eighths of an inch.

Ditto on right side, one inch and one-eighth.

From the inner surface of the pubes, anteriorly, to the acetabulum on the right side, three inches and seven-eighths.

Ditto, left side, three inches and four-eighths.

Cross measure of the widest portion of the anterior slit, five-eighths of an inch.

Ditto at the point of the widest portion of the anterior slit, two-eighths of an inch.

Outlet—From the point of the coccyx to the lower edge of the symphysis pubis, two inches and five-eighths.

From the widest part of the anterior slit to the coccyx, one inch and two-eighths.

Depth of the anterior slit, two inches.

Between the anterior edges of the tubera ischii, one inch and six-eighths.

Ditto, posterior edges of the tubera ischii, two inches and four-eighths.

From the right spine of ischium to the coccyx, six-eighths of an inch.

Ditto, left spine of ischium to the coccyx, five-eighths of an inch.

Depth of the fore part of the pelvis, three inches and five-eighths.

Ditto of lateral part of the pelvis, three inches and six-eighths.

Ditto of posterior part of the pelvis, three inches.

Distance, externally, between the bottoms of the acetabula, one inch and seven-eighths.

Ditto, internal measurement, one inch and three-eighths.

Ditto between the superior spinous processes of the ilii, seven inches and a half.

Ditto between the inferior spinous processes of the ilii, four inches and seven-eighths.

Ditto between the centre of the crests of the ilii, ten inches.

Ditto from the upper edge of the fourth lumbar vertebra to the inferior spinous process of right ilium, one inch and six-eighths.

Ditto, of left ilium, two inches and six-eighths (see sketch, fig. 3).

Remarks.—Mollities ossium, under which this woman suffered, usually commences during pregnancy; but in her case it most likely began at the time she first complained of pains in the back and hips. The disease now most probably made little progress until her second pregnancy, when no doubt it was much aggravated; but its ravages on the pelvic bones were chiefly made during her last gestation.

Some of her relations had suffered from rheumatism, and it was stated that she had laboured under the same complaint; but for anything I know to the contrary, they (her relations) might have had the disease now under consideration. The predisposition, then (most likely hereditary), remained comparatively undisturbed until roused into activity by those changes which are produced on the vascular and absorbent system by impregnation. Her occupation as a weaver no doubt greatly contributed to increase the degree of pelvic distortion.

The projection of the promontory of the sacrum and lumbar vertebræ mechanically impeded the passage of the fœces into the rectum—which in such cases is always an additional cause of constipation—and which almost invariably occur to a greater or less degree in ordinary pregnancies.

The enema apparatus should have a long flexible tube (like that used to throw fluids into the stomach), so that its point can be carried beyond the altered pelvic brim.

An ordinary female catheter is too short to answer its purpose in cases of this sort; it should be equal in length to that of the male. By the deflected state of the uterus, the bladder is forced forwards and downwards, whereby its cervix is lengthened and compressed upon the pubes. This altered position of the bladder requires a different method to pass the instrument. The point being introduced into the meatus (which lies in the upper part of the anterior pelvic slit, and a little behind the lower part of the symphysis pubis) the hand part must then be depressed and carried backwards towards the extremity of the coccyx, and the instrument must afterwards be cautiously moved on into the bladder.

The stethoscope affords us information of two kinds—positive and negative; in its application here we only derived the latter kind. The pulsation of the infant's heart could not be heard, and from the absence of its sound, coupled with the odour of the vaginal discharge, we concluded it was dead. The functions of the placenta had long ceased; and therefore no *soufflet placentaire* was audible, so as to point out to us the location of this organ. If it had been otherwise, I might, and indeed ought, as far as possible, to have made the incision into the uterus so as to avoid cutting on and into the placenta. The importance of such a procedure I had stated before the operation, to Mr. Dunn, and requested that he would, as expeditiously as possible, extract the infant, and at the same time pass one hand to guard its neck from spasmodic seizure by the uterus, if perchance I should unfortunately cut upon the placenta.

I have elsewhere (*Edin. Med. and Surg. Journal,* vol. 60 and 67) ventured to state this (the incision, and consequent partial separation of the placenta) as a cause of this irregular contraction of the uterus. If the child had been alive, most likely such a grasp would have destroyed it before it could have been extricated.

It is to be lamented that the existence of labour had not been earlier known; perhaps a different termination would have taken place. To wait for the changes which usually occur in the os uteri during the first stage of normal labour is a great mistake in those cases in which there exists great pelvic distortion.

This part of the uterus is not often to be felt, and when it is accessible it is found a little open; its full dilatation having been prevented by the vicious conformation of the brim of the pelvis. The evil arising from this procrastination ought to be a beacon to us in future, and guard us against vainly waiting for such a change.

The highly inflamed state of the bowels, which existed before the operation, and their pathological condition after death, together with that of the os and cervix uteri, etc., afforded indisputable evidence of the mischief which had been inflicted during her protracted labour.

The term protraction should be relatively considered. A woman (as in this case) in a bad state of health cannot safely endure the same degree of pain, or for the same length of time, as one who is well ; nor will the os and cervix uteri bear pressure very long without structural injury. Surely there is here sufficient proof of the necessity of the Cæsarean section : for neither the presentation of the infant, nor the os uteri, could be touched. Independent of these circumstances, I am bold to assert, the delivery could not have been performed by the perforator and crochet, even if assisted by the marvellous power of the osteotomist, provided the implements were used by the most experienced and celebrated anti-Cæsareanist. No practitioner, then, however warped his opinions are, will presume to attribute the death of this poor creature to the operation ; but, on the contrary, will place the case in the catalogue (already too great) of those in which the death has happened in consequence of having too long deferred its performance.

CASE (Tab.) 42 (*Unsuccessful*). I am enabled to lay before the profession the following interesting case, through the kindness of the brother of the late Dr. Hardy, who had promised to give it me previous to his death :—

" Betty Wilcock, the subject of the following operation, was within a few weeks of completing her forty-ninth year, as appears from the baptismal register, dated October 26th, 1776. Her general health was good until within the last seven years, during which she experienced a dull heavy pain in the back and hips, and felt herself gradually growing weaker. Five years ago she consulted me respecting the pain in .the loins; she was advised to take laxatives, with mercurial alteratives, and afterwards to try the sea air, from which she derived considerable benefit. Her health was best during the summer months, the pain and weakness always increasing on the approach of winter; she decreased several inches in stature; and walked with considerable difficulty, and for the last two months of her pregnancy she was carried to and from bed. She was the mother of ten children, the youngest of whom was six years of age, and I was informed her labour at that time was more lingering and protracted than any she had previously experienced. I had not seen her from the time she consulted me about the pain in her loins, until I was requested to attend her in labour. The pains commenced on Tuesday night (June 25th, 1825), and, continuing, she sent for me about twelve o'clock on Wednesday night. Being engaged, my senior apprentice went and remained with her until Thursday noon, when I visited her, I found that the membranes had ruptured spontaneously, and the water dribbled away ; the pains came on regularly every six or eight minutes. On making an ordinary examination, I could not reach the child, and, on trying to introduce my hand, experienced great difficulty. The tubera ischii approached each other within an inch and a half ; the angle formed by the ossa pubis was very acute, and from the tuber ischii to the symphysis might be about three inches. On carrying my hand flat between the rami of the pubes, I could introduce it above six inches, and found the child's head presenting, with a portion of the funis. The superior aperture was very small ; the junction of the two last lumbar vertebræ, with the os sacrum, projected into the cavity of the pelvis, so that the antero-posterior diameter did not appear more than one inch and a quarter.

Over this projection, and on the symphysis pubis, the head of the child lay. The pulsation in the funis was very strong. Though she had been in labour for more than forty hours, she had no fever. Pulse 84; tongue coated with a brown crust, but quite moist. At eleven o'clock, finding the labour did not proceed, and her strength declining, I sent for Mr. Hardy, of Whalley (a gentleman who had extensively practised the different branches of the profession for upwards of thirty years). He arrived about one o'clock on Friday morning, and, on a very careful examination, found everything as above detailed, and agreed with me on the impossibility of delivering the woman with the crochet. On explaining to her the circumstances of her case, and the necessity of having recourse to the Cæsarean section, as the only means of affording her relief, she willingly acceded to it. At three o'clock A.M., Friday, I sent for Dr. Martland, of Blackburn, who carefully examined the patient, and fully agreed with Mr. Hardy and myself on the propriety of performing the Cæsarean operation. The bowels having been freely moved by an injection, and the bladder emptied, and the necessary preparation being made, at seven A.M. the patient was placed on the table. The abdomen was very pendulous, and rested upon her thighs. Dr. Martland placed his hands on each side, and firmly supported it. I commenced the incision through the integuments, beginning about an inch and a half below the umbilicus, and extended it down the linea alba, to within two inches of the symphysis pubis, making it six inches in length. The parietes of the abdomen were very thin, and the uterus was seen rolling through the peritoneum, which being divided by the probe-pointed bistoury, the uterus was fully exposed, and appeared of a light rosy colour ; I commenced the incision into the uterus a little above the cervix, and carried it for the space of five inches towards the fundus, being as cautious as possible in avoiding the large sinuses. The cut surface of the uterus was fully half an inch thick. A large bag of water, of a pale whey colour, immediately protruded, which, on being opened, discharged about sixteen ounces. The left arm of a child now presented, and it was easily extracted, and soon was very lively. Very soon after the delivery of this, the right leg of another made its appearance, covered by the membrane, through which a quantity of meconium was seen. This child was also delivered, and shortly after birth exhibited signs of animation. This was the child that presented its head and funis over the superior aperture of the pelvis. The apex of the head was corrugated and contracted into a small cone, its circumference scarcely exceeding two inches and a quarter, a very moderate hæmorrhage succeeded the extraction of the placenta. The divided edges of the uterus which now appeared above an inch in thickness, were brought together and kept in close apposition for a short time ; and so great was the contraction that, in a few seconds, the wound did not exceed half its former size. Through the firm and judicious support of the abdomen and uterus, none of the intestines were seen ; the former was closed by the Glover's suture ; long slips of adhesive plaster were applied ; and a many-tailed bandage, made of flannel, was firmly bound round the body. During the operation, the patient was rather faint; but a little weak brandy and water revived her, after which she was removed into bed. The pulse was 108, and tolerably full ; there was a plentiful discharge of lochia, and she expressed herself very comfortable. I visited her with Mr. Hardy about half-past eleven A.M., and found she had been quite easy since the operation. Her tongue was moist, but coated with a light-brown crust; pulse 104. She had no pain or tenderness in the abdomen; had a very plentiful discharge of lochia; but she experienced slight pains in the uterus, resembling after-pains. I ordered her to take the simple saline effervescing drafts every two hours.

Half-past seven P.M. I visited her with Dr. Martland. Pulse 120, tolerably strong and regular; tongue rather dry, but not furred. She had comfortable perspiration during the day; complained of a twitching extending from the epigastric region to the right shoulder. She had passed urine since the operation. There was no distention of the abdomen, nor any particular pain on pressure; a plentiful discharge of lochia. I introduced the catheter, and extracted sixteen and a half ounces of urine, after which she felt relieved.

℞ Sol. acet. morph. ℳviij; aquæ puræ ʒj. M. Ft. haust. h. s. s.
℞ Hydr. sub. gr. 4; pulv. ipecac. co. ϴj; pot. nitr. ℨiss. M. et
    div. in pulveris viij; quoram sumat i 6tis horis.
    Cont. mist. sol. efferv. ut antea.

July 2nd, seven A.M. In the early part of the night she had a great deal of pain in her bowels, constant, but not resembling after-pains. The uneasiness about the stomach had left her, and she slept at intervals during the night, and continued to perspire gently. About twelve o'clock she vomited a little sour water, by which she was relieved. Lochia plentiful. Catheter introduced, and about ten ounces of urine drawn off. Pulse 120, strong and regular; tongue moist and coated with a slight brownish fur. Through the neglect of her attendant, the draught was given in divided doses, and the powders were omitted. Inspiration 26 per minute; feels quite comfortable; abdomen free from pain.

℞ Magn. sulph. ʒiij; mag. carb. ϴj; inf. senn. ʒiiss. M. Ft.
    mist. cujus sumr. cochl. ij, quâqu. horâ donec alv. resp.
    Cont. mist. sal. efferves.

7 P.M. She had been tolerably easy since morning, but had experienced slight twitching pains, extending from the stomach to the uterus. Pulse 120, rather full; tongue moist, but coated with a little brownish crust. She had a slight cough, which gave her much uneasiness in the left hypogastric region. Lochia copious. Abdomen rather more painful on pressure, and more distended, evidently with flatus. Catheter introduced; only six ounces of urine were discharged. The opening medicine was not given according to direction, and the powders were again omitted. An enema was administered, which moved her bowels freely, and gave relief.

July 3rd. I was called to her about half-past one A.M. She had been seized with sickness, and ejected some brown water from her stomach, which came up in mouthfuls, and caused her much pain in the epigastric region. She was considerably relieved by bleeding. The tenderness in the abdomen abated and pulse 120, more feeble. The blood had a very thick inflammatory coat, and was cupped. To take five drops of sol. morph. each hour. Emplast. lyttæ reg. epigast. applic.

11 A.M. Sickness left her soon after taking the drops. She remained tolerably easy, and slumbered. Had a few of the twitchings from the stomach to the uterus. Not much tenderness felt on making pressure, but abdomen more distended, and, on being struck with the finger, had a tympanitic sound; pulse 130, feeble and inter-

mitting; countenance lost its animation; catheter introduced, and about five ounces of urine extracted; bowels not moved.

℞ Hydr. submur. gr. vj; extr. col. c. 3ss. M. Pil. vj. Cap. j sec. quâque horâ.

5 P.M. Soon after I left her the regurgitation of water from the stomach returned. She became more restless; pulse fluttered, and was very feeble; her hands were covered with a cold clammy sweat, and she appeared to be fast sinking.

7 P.M. In a state of stupor, from which she could be roused, and would give sensible answers to any question, but soon relapsed.

She expired about half-past eight—sixty-one and a half hours after the operation. The children feed very well, and are in perfect health."

REMARKS. The foregoing case is unique—at least in Great Britain and Ireland—in the annals of medical literature. It affords an example of the preservation of the lives of two infants; and, if the operation had been earlier performed, and the after-treatment strictly adapted to the exigences of the case, most probably the mother might also have been saved. These twins were girls, and most likely arrived at womanhood; as it is stated, in an appended paper to details of the case, they presented themselves for confirmation after they had passed their sixteenth year.

Betty Wilcock had borne ten children, and, in all but one, her labours were natural and easy; this, the last, was protracted; so that it may be supposed the pelvis had at this period suffered in its conformation. The disease which caused the pelvic deformity was malacosteon, which evidently at first slowly advanced, mainly owing to the long interval (six years) between her last (tenth) and this (her eleventh) labour. Gestation invariably aggravates this disease; hence the increased relative difficulties experienced in successive labours in cases in which it exists.

There is no positive pathological evidence what caused her death, as no *post mortem* examination was made; but from the symptoms and treatment we may suspect that inflammation of the peritoneum, or some of the abdominal viscera, had taken place.

The duration of her labour (eighty-three hours) is quite sufficient to produce all the mischief which ensued; and the result affords another striking example of the danger of procrastinating the operation. The suture (Glover's) used is not suitable to close the abdominal wound during life; and though unwilling to make any observation which tends in the least degree to detract from the character of the operator, yet it is a duty to warn others against a practice fraught with danger: it must decidedly tend to injure the peritoneum.

CASE (Tab.) 49 (*Successful*). At half-past one o'clock A.M., Thursday, November 20th, 1845, I visited Mrs. Sankey, Bedford Street, Salford, who was then in labour. I met Mr. John Goodman, from whom I learnt the case was one of extreme distortion of the pelvis, etc. She first felt slight pains about eleven o'clock on Wednesday morning. Sometimes they were stronger, and continued to vary in severity until about three hours before my arrival, during which time they were uniformly stronger. The membranes ruptured some time in the afternoon, and there was a slight dribbling discharge at intervals, up to the time of my first visit. The tongue was clean and moist; her countenance was calm and composed; her bowels had been freely evacuated; and she had regularly discharged her urine;

she was free from sickness and vomiting ; pulse 84 at first, but temporarily rose to 100. Placing my hand upon the abdomen, I found
the uterus of a spheroidal shape, but less so than I had observed in
former cases : it felt firm and free from pain, when I pressed upon
it. The relative position of this organ was now much altered : it
hung over, and rested on the pubes ; and the fundus projected so
much forward as to actually form its anterior surface. Connected
with, and in reference to, the axis of the vagina, it presented the retort form. By a vaginal examination, I found the outlet of the
pelvis considerably diminished by the close approximation of the
rami of the ischii and pubes, which jutting forward, had nearly destroyed the arch, and leaving in its place only a narrow slit which
would barely admit the point of the finger. The tubera ischia were
so near as scarcely to allow two fingers to lie in the transverse
diameter; the antero-posterior was also much shortened by the great
incurvation of the coccyx and lower portion of the sacrum. The
cavity was diminished by the several bones which unite in each acetabulum being forced inwards, backwards, and upwards. It was
difficult to measure the brim ; its figure was tripartite.

This alteration in shape was produced by the falling down of the
promontory of the sacrum and lumbar vertebræ, and by the ischia
and pubes being pushed backwards and inwards, and the jutting
forwards of the symphysis and rami of the pubes. The antero-
posterior diameter was not more than an inch and a half at its widest
part on the right side, and in some parts not an inch. The anterior
lobe of the opening was not more than would admit the finger edgeways (see sketch, fig. 4). The vagina was moist, and had only its
natural temperature; it was free from swelling. The os uteri, or
the presentation of the infant, could not be felt.

On returning down stairs to Mr. Goodman, I cordially agreed with
him that the Cæsarean section was the only means by which delivery
could be performed. I suggested the propriety of having the stethoscope applied to testify whether the infant was alive, as the mother
affirmed, and also to ascertain the location of the placenta. At this
stage I also requested that Mr. Winterbottom, surgeon, should be
invited. A messenger (Mr. S.) was despatched for Mr. Winterbottom, who was desired to bring with him a stethoscope. I now
remarked on the danger of cutting into and partially separating the
placenta during the operation. Auscultation indicated that this
organ was attached to the anterior and right lateral portion of the
uterus, and corroborated the statements made by the patient that
the infant was alive.

I now raised the fundus uteri, and Mr. Goodman made an incision, from seven to eight inches long, a little to the left of the
umbilicus, and divided the integuments, which were extremely thin.
A corresponding opening was now made through the uterine tissue,
which was about a quarter or one-third of an inch in thickness, just
bordering on the edge of the placenta. I now passed my hand, and
seized one leg of the infant, and extracted it ; and when it passed to
the head, Mr. Goodman assisted its escape through the wound, and
afterwards expeditiously extracted the placenta entire. The infant
—a girl—was alive. There was very little blood indeed lost, and the
uterus contracted and lowered itself to its resting-place. The intestines and omentum protruded during the operation, but were then

---

* See Figure 4th.

restrained, and afterwards replaced and retained in their natural position during the time the ligatures were introduced. I swept my finger round the boundary of the uterus, and through the wound in its cavity, to ascertain if any portion of the viscera had got into it. The interrupted suture was used, and the thin integuments further brought together by strips of adhesive plaister; and over all a bandage just tight enough to give support was applied. There was a calmness and resignation of mind throughout the whole operation which indicated an enduring Christian spirit. No complaint was made, nor murmur heard ; and she expressed herself as happily relieved.

The pulse now beat 92. She had a little gulping ; the skin felt warm. Habeat tr. opii ʒiss ; in one or two hours pulse 94 ; slight retching ; and a very trifling oozing of blood was seen on the bandage ; her lips were naturally red; respiration 26. Fresh bandage and a compress applied. At a quarter-past nine o'clock a.m., tongue clean ; countenance natural ; respiration 24 ; about two or three ounces of blood lost ; a negative plan recommended—mist. acac. ʒi, vel. ʒiss—ter in die.

Eight o'clock vespere. Pulse reduced from 100 to 90; countenance good ; had complained of tightness of the bandage ; the belly a little tumefied, but not tender ; there is no bleeding. To take ext. hyoscyam. gr. x.

November 21st, ten o'clock a.m. Had vomited a sour fluid during the night. Pulse 86; countenance natural; tongue clean and smooth; skin cool ; lochial discharge natural ; bowels not moved ; had passed her urine. Ordered an enema as follows :—Spt. terebinth. r. ʒij ; ol. ricini ʒj ; vitelli ovi q. s. et aq. hord.

Half-past one o'clock P.M. Tongue clean; she has vomited a dark-coloured thick and sour fluid, which in appearance looks like fæces. Enema has not operated ; ordered to be repeated : to take barley water.

Nine o'clock, vespere. Has had no stool ; vomiting continues ; belly tympanitic. The compress being removed, the site of the lower portion of the abdominal wound was tumid, and on raising the plaister the wound itself was seen gaping, and a fold or convolution of intestine had protruded between (in the interstices of) the two ligatures. The bandage and plaister was now removed. An attempt was made to reduce the bowel, and the edges of the wound well adapted, and fresh strips of plaister and a three-tailed bandage applied. Ordered, at her request, ol. ricini f. ʒss : to be repeated if necessary.

22nd, nine o'clock A.M. Had some sleep; pulse 100; had vomited the oil, and also some of the same fluid ; tongue clean ; belly less swelled, but slightly sore ; there is a considerable bloody serous discharge from the wound; has passed urine; lochial discharge; has had no stool. To take calomel gr. v ; a quantity of gruel to be thrown up by the syringe with the œsophagus tube passed high up towards the sigmoid flexure of the colon.

Seven o'clock, vespere. Has slept several times ; pulse 90 to 95 ; feels better ; skin cool ; vomiting ceased ; belly less swelled, and easy ; another enema had been administered, but it procured no stool. Ordered calomel gr. v ; sacch. alb. gr. vss.

℞ Magnes. sulph. ʒvj ; magnes. calcinat. ʒij; tr. cardam. comp. ʒj ; aq. cinnam. ʒiij. Coch. larg. j 3tiis horis. Repr. dos. anod. noct.

23rd, ten o'clock A.M. She had slept; pulse 90; tongue clean; had vomited only once a light-coloured fluid; bowels opened four times; skin warm and perspiring; very slight abdominal uneasiness.

Five o'clock, vespere. Had visited her before, and found her going on well: a considerable serous discharge from the wound; had not vomited; has had three stools; passed urine; has had several sleeps. To continue mist. acac. et cætera.

24th, ten o'clock A.M. Pulse 95; tongue clean, but redder in the centre; has very little abdominal pain on pressure; bowels purged two or three times; has passed urine; says she feels weak. Pergat. To take beef-tea.

Half-past seven o'clock, vespere. Pulse 100; tongue clean, but sore; belly less tumefied, and bears pressure; a considerable bloody serous discharge from the wound; had been twice purged, attended with griping pain. To continue the medicine; also to take half an ounce of the following mixture if the diarrhœa continues, and also to take one pill:—

℞ Cretæ ʒj; mist. acac. ℥iss; aq. dest. ℥j; tinct. opii ʒj. M. ft.
℞ Opii gr. ss; conf. arom. q. s. fiat pil. h. s. s.

Nov. 25th, ten o'clock A.M. Pulse 94; tongue clean; had slept; lochial discharge natural; had passed urine; bowels not again moved; gentle perspiration; belly easy. Pergat. Ordered chicken broth.

Half-past four P.M. Pulse 85; symptoms all favourable; has a cough: taken freely of chicken broth and beef-tea. Ext. hyoscyam. gr. x h. s. ℞ Mist. acaciæ ℥ij; tr. camph. co. ʒiij; syrup. rhœad. ℥ss. M. fiat. tinct. cujus cap. cochl. ℳj sub urgent. tuss.

26th, ten o'clock, A.M. Pulse 95; tongue clean; skin a little hotter; bowels unmoved and tympanitic; had passed urine; her countenance a little more anxious. The bandage and plaister were removed; the ligatures were detached from their hold; the integuments expanded to such a degree as to present a large surface of the bowels, which were uniformly covered with lymph; the incised edges were firmly agglutinated to the contiguous parts; attempts were made to bring the integumental edges nearer together, and the bowels were gently pushed back, and broad straps of adhesive plaister were tightly applied, and a six-tailed bandage, so as to afford firm and equal support. Ordered Mist. magnes. sulph. ʒvj; magnes. calcin. ʒij; aq. ℥vj; cujus cap. ℥j tertiis horis donec alv. resp.; and the following form of enema to be administered if necessary:—

℞ Sp. terebinth. ℥ij; tinct. assafœt. ʒij; aq. ℥vss: to be added to ℥viij of barley water.

Six o'clock, vespere. Pulse 120; skin hotter; has great depression; tongue dry; countenance anxious; bowels unmoved; complains of pain in the belly; had passed water. Ordered the enema to be immediately thrown up. She has just vomited. Pergat. An anodyne to be prescribed.

27th. Took morph. acet. gr. ½ cum ext. pap. gr. iij. She has had four motions; has slept well; and generally better. Pulse 90 to 96. Cont. mist. acac. tinct.; beef-tea; and take anodyne at bed-time.

28th. Pulse 96; has slept well; has had two motions; a considerable discharge from the wound; all the other symptoms better except the cough, which is rather more troublesome. Continue medicine and diet—and take isinglass.

29th. Pulse 84 to 90; slept well; bowels twice naturally moved; all the symptoms more favourable; a considerable discharge on the bandage. Upon removing the bandage and dressings, the wound presented a healthy granulating surface, and covered with pure pus. There was a small slough at the lower edge. The integuments below, in the bend of the thigh, were irritated and excoriated by the discharge. Continue diet and medicines.

30th. Pulse 86 to 100; tongue clean and smooth; bowels moved. Complains of sore throat, which is red, and slightly aphthous. Cough very troublesome, and, from its force, produces a sensation of forcing some part through the wound, and, on examination, a portion of bowel was found protruded. The lower part of the bandage and dressing being now removed, the wound was seen not to be so well; the granulations were paler; the discharge from the left was blackish from the slough. Fresh pledget of lint and plaister applied. Continue the same medicine and diet, and also to have eggs, and the following mixture:—

℞ Sodæ sub-borat. pulv. bone ℨiij; syrup. rhœad. ℨss; mist. acaciæ ℨijss. M. cujus capiat paululum subinde.

℞ Morph. acet. gr. ¼; ext. pap. alb. gr. iij. Fiat pil. h. s. s. et rep. in horis 2 si op. sit.

December 1st. Pulse 100; all other general symptoms better. A considerable discharge from the sore, which was dark-coloured and offensive; a protrusion of the granulated portion of the sore through the dressings, which were now removed. The aspect of sore pale; its left edge was sloughy in places. The dressings were changed, and pledgets of lint with cerate over. Double folds of linen were placed, and a six-tailed bandage, to support as far as possible. Our object was to form a barrier to further protrusion, as, from the intimate adhesion which now existed among the convolutions of the bowels themselves, and between them and the integuments, it would be mischievous to attempt to do more than barely to defend and to support these parts. On the right side, the old and the new surface presented one plane. To take a generous diet, and porter; and also the anodyne pill.

2nd. All the general symptoms favourable. Had first refused to take porter, but afterwards did so. Wound looks better; granulations redder; pus laudable; cicatrisation on left side proceeding; sloughing appearance on the right side much better. Continue diet, porter, and a night-pill. At the evening visit she reported she had taken a beefsteak at dinner, and porter; and we found her eating the leg of a fowl, and again drinking porter. Cautions given not to get into excess.

3rd. Mr. Goodman, at a later visit last night, found her pulse considerably more frequent. She complained of the wound. On examination he discovered that a large loop of intestine had protruded on the left side, which he unsuccessfully attempted to reduce. He placed a pledget of lint with cerate over it. This morning the pulse 120; bowels not moved; she had vomited some undigested animal food. The body linen was very wet by discharge, which had a pungent disagreeable smell; the dressings adhered so firmly that they were with difficulty removed. A loop of intestine, of a horseshoe shape, covered with lymph, and fixed by adhesion; it was very much distended. Cautious but unsuccessful attempts were made to reduce it. I suggested the propriety to puncture it with a needle; a sharp pointed bistoury was however used, but nothing but a little blood escaped. Another unsuccessful attempt was made to reduce it. Broad slips of plaister and a bandage applied. An enema, with oil, etc., to be thrown up with the syringe and œsophagus tube. To discontinue the porter and animal food ; to take chicken broth. Ordered some coriander or mustard seed to be taken, and the anodyne pills.

4th. Bowels freely moved several times, but the seeds were not seen ; all the symptoms better. Continue.

5th. Bowels three times moved, and in the last motion the coriander seeds were seen ; every other general symptom favourable. The wound healthy ; the union on the right side complete, and the cicatrisation proceeding : on the left side the loop of the bowel still lay prominent, and the edges of the sore were everted, and in an un-favourable position for this reparative process. Continue diet and anodyne pills.

6th. Pulse 96 ; bowels unmoved ; slept well ; wound looking healthy, and lessening in diameter; cicatrisation rapidly proceeding; the surface over the protruded intestine loop granulating ; this por-tion of the bowel immoveably fixed down. Continue medicine and diet ; to have an enema and her anodyne pills.

7th. Pulse 90 ; bowels twice very freely moved, and in one motion some coriander seeds were found ; a profuse irritating dis-charge through the dressing. On exposing the parts, an opening was found at the lower end of the protruded bowel, through which fæces had passed, and were now escaping. The enema had not been given, but it was now directed to be administered. To continue to take the anodyne.

8th. Pulse 90 ; slept well ; bowels once opened by the enema. The size of the wound is considerably diminished, and its surface looking healthy. Fæces in great abundance were discharged through the intestinal opening. To continue the same plan. Ordered an enema and anodyne pills.

9th. Pulse 84; bowels opened by enema; the wound is diminished in size, and looks healthy. The fæces are largely discharged through the opening in the bowel. To continue ; to try to eat some calf's foot ; to have an enema and the anodyne.

10th. Pulse 80 to 84 ; the wound considerably lessened, and its entire surface looks well. The apparent size of the protruded bowel is greatly diminished, and is covered with healthy granulations ; its horse-shoe character is nearly lost. Great quantity of feculent matter comes through the opening ; portion of undigested calf's foot was observed in the discharge. Ordered a little wine. Con-tinue diet ; to have an enema and pill.

11th. Pulse 74 ; wound lessened, and looks well ; bowels moved by enema; fæces in great abundance from the opening. To continue wine, etc.

12th. Pulse 72 ; had two stools, which were too light in colour, which perhaps depends upon the escape of the biliary fluid too soon, as the fæcal discharge by the opening has been all along very deeply tinged, and is still in great quantity. The sore is now considerably lessened ; it does not measure more than four inches in length, and two to two and a half inches in breadth. The protruded intestine so far retired as not to be seen, except when the integument is drawn aside. The integumental edges of the sore can now be approximated. To continue the wine, etc. ; to have an enema ; to take a pill.

13th. Pulse 74; right edge of the wound was more inverted, and which had been produced by approximating the two sides; bowels slightly moved; considerable fæcal discharge from the wound, and in it some coriander seeds were seen, which had been taken early in the day. The wound dressed in its longitudinal direction. Continue the wine, etc.; to have an enema; to take the pills.

14th. Pulse 72; has had no motion; granulations paler; the discharge of fæcal matter greater through the wound; a sponge compress was applied over the opening, which was to be removed at intervals; it was, however, permanently discontinued in the evening. Continue the wine. To have jelly, blancmange, isinglass, and to be allowed a partridge.

15th. Pulse 76; small hard fragment of stool brought with the enema; countenance more dejected; complains this morning of a load at the stomach, which, in the course of the day, ended in vomiting of a quantity of undigested animal food; the fæcal discharge great from the wound; as the granulations were exuberant, the sore was dressed with dry lint. Wine increased; continue altera.

16th. Pulse 74; wound less, and looks better; bowels not moved. To only have some broth, with a little of the chicken pounded in it. Continue medicine; to have an enema.

20th. No particular change in the aspect of the case up to this date. Pulse now 74; the fæces still largely discharged from the intestinal opening; the protruded portion of bowel very red from the everted mucous membrane. Mr. G. passed his little finger, and carried this part in; a compress was applied, and supported by plaister.

31st. During the interval, the pulse nearly uniformly 72. Bowels some days spontaneously moved once or twice; but, nevertheless, an enema was daily administered. All the general symptoms continued to improve, and the excoriations produced by the discharge were attended to by washing, etc. The everted mucous membrane of the bowel which appeared through the opening had at first rather increased, but now was considerably less. Compresses or pads were applied, etc. The discharge of fæcal matter through the opening had gradually lessened.

January 10th, 1846. As in the last report, the pulse had uniformly continued steady. The bowels were sometimes moved more than once a day; the enemas were regularly administered; the everted state of the mucous membrane of the bowel varied in degree and colour. Her spirits were very low on the 4th, in consequence of the very great discharge which took place through the opening in the bowel. The treatment consisted of small pads placed immediately over the aperture, being supported by small slips of adhesive plaister, and then, upon the integuments and over the other, a larger pad, etc., fixed by broad straps and a bandage.

17th. Since the last report the pulse continued natural, and she slept well, and her appetite was good. The bowels were naturally opened once or twice a day, and therefore the enema had been discontinued until the 14th ult., when the bowels being only partially moved, and as the belly had become more tumid, they were again used. The discharge from the intestinal opening was at first less solid and more serous, but afterwards it became again more feculent. Compresses of different kinds were applied, and one suggested by me made of layers of caoutchouc was used, but did not succeed. On this day the fæcal discharge was much greater, which I accounted for by the opening, which was about the size of a silver fourpenny-piece, having changed its relative position with the integuments. I recommended that a conical piece of sponge should be placed with its point inwards, and supported by plaister and bandage. Mr. Goodman feared that it would be injurious to use the sponge, as it might dilate the opening and induce ulceration. My reply was, that I did not fear the first effect ; and if the second happened, it would only be limited in degree, and advantageous. I thought at this time the edges of the wound were in a favourable position to be pared, and a ligature used to bring them into apposition.

22nd. Pulse kept natural, and the bowels were daily moved twice. The sponge had become a little swelled, and the edges of the opening bled a little. It was re-applied on the 20th. The bandage was very wet, and was attended by a disagreeable ammoniacal smell, which no doubt arose from the decomposition of the discharged fluid, which had taken place in consequence of the parts not having been dressed the day before. The surrounding integuments were considerably irritated and excoriated. At my desire, a simple dressing with lint and cerate was adopted, and a very loose bandage applied. The patient sat up, but the horizontal position was advised. On this day (22nd) the eversion of the mucous membrane was greater and the opening had slightly increased. A piece of sponge was recommended by me, but a compress of lint was applied at Mr. Goodman's desire.

23rd. Pulse good ; bowels twice moved ; the integumental excoriation rather extended ; the intestinal opening is a little larger. Mr. Goodman proposed touching its edges with argent. nitrat.; but I considered that the surface would heal underneath before the eschar separated, and suggested the potass. fusa. Mr. Goodman thought it would be difficult to limit its application, although my opinion was that its action might be controlled. I recommended instead of it, the edges of the opening to be pared off, which Mr. Goodman did by a lancet and bistoury. This operation was not so effectually done, in consequence of the tender and fragile state of the part. The edges were approximated, and supported by slips of adhesive plaster. The integuments being drawn together, formed a covering and compress to the aperture.

31st. During this interval the pulse was natural, and the bowels some days moved spontaneously, and always responded to the use of an enema. The intestinal opening remained much the same ; and the discharge from it, although not equal in amount every day, yet it was sometimes very great. Various methods were tried to control it : pitch plasters in different ways, and compresses, were used at the suggestion of Mr. Goodman, but they invariably failed to do good ; on the contrary, mischief was done by them. At my request, pads made from caoutchouc, of different sizes, and placed differently, were employed, but equally unsuccessfully. I recommended broad straps of plaster from the Infirmary to be tried, which also failed. As considerable irritation and excoriation had been produced by the pitch plaster,—indeed, the pain and inconvenience sustained by the patient was such that she not only requested a discontinuance, but strongly protested against its use,—my opinion was unfavourable to their use, as I considered disadvantages from these arose, not only on account of the irritation, etc., arising from the pitch itself, but from the mechanical effects, by inflecting the integuments upon each other and also by impeding, by the great pressure produced, the peristaltic motion of the bowels. On the 30th, I saw the patient alone, and thought it would be better to apply a simple dressing.

February 1st to 13th. It appears that a great discharge issued from the opening after the last dressing; so that the nurse, at the desire of Mrs. Sankey, had removed them, and brought the edges together by adhesive plaster. Long strips of plaster were again recommended by Mr. G., and very tightly applied, some of which were passed round from one side of the spine to the other.

Great integumental irritation and excoriation ensued, and it was therefore thought desirable not to bind the parts so tightly. The edges of the opening were touched from time to time with the argent. nitrat. On February 2nd, I suggested the propriety of having a bandage made of some elastic but firm material, so that the diaphragm and abdominal muscles could move in opposite directions without the least impediment, and at the same time afford uniform support.

11th. Mrs. Sankey stated that they had removed the quill, as nothing had passed through it. Mr. Goodman had placed the barrel of a quill as a conductor for the fæcal discharge; but this, it appears, did not answer, nor was it likely to do so, as it would be quite impossible to place such a body in a parallel direction with the course of the intestinal tube; and we cannot for a moment suppose that it could act by suction.

12th. I found that pitch had been used again in dressing the part the day before. The evils were increased by this plan: the surrounding irritation and excoriation were seen to be much greater. Mr. Goodman ordered a new bandage, with gussets for the hips; and buckles and straps were attached to it, so that it could be tightened and fixed. This contrivance proved of great advantage to her. She wore it a considerable time, and Mr. Goodman states he had the satisfaction to find a progressive diminution of the fæcal discharge, which passed through the intestinal aperture.

REMARKS. Mrs. Sankey's occupation was merely domestic; she was a slender, delicate, and spare-looking woman. Her complexion was pale; her skin was swarthy; her eyes were grey; and she was of a leucophlegmatic constitution. She was naturally of a mild and placid disposition; and her mind was placable and strongly imbued with sound, moral, and religious principles, which wonderfully supported her in her severe trial, the intensity of which it is scarcely possible for imagination to conceive. What can be more dreadful than the anxieties of a woman in the pangs of labour without hope of delivery? She bore the operation with great fortitude, and scarcely made a moan; and afterwards endured a tedious recovery with great patience and resignation.

Her age was 41 years. This was her seventh pregnancy. Her first four labours were natural and easy: in the first, she was delivered of a living girl; and, in the other three, of boys—all born alive. Her fifth labour was natural, but it was rather more tedious than her former ones: the infant (a boy) was born alive. At the end of two years she was again in labour of her sixth child, which was protracted by pelvic distortion; and Mr. Goodman, with Mr. Slack's assistance, delivered her by means of the perforator and crochet.

The disease (mollities ossium) under which she now suffered, no doubt commenced after her fifth labour, which proved a little tedious.

It is, however, very probable that the mischief inflicted on the pelvis was only slight at this period : and, during the interval between it and her next pregnancy, most likely the disease remained stationary. Whilst pregnant of her sixth child it rapidly advanced, and committed great ravages in the pelvis. Her general health suffered and her strength failed ; her stature became obviously less. Mr. Goodman kindly informed me the thighs somewhat bowed, but afterwards recovered the usual shape. During her labour, Mr. Goodman found the pelvic diameter shortened ; the antero-posterior only measured about two inches.

After a consultation with Mr. Slack, he delivered her with the perforator and crochet ; it, however, rarely happens that the disease is so rapid in its progress, and does so much injury to the pelvis, as to require these murderous instruments before those which are compatible with the safety of the infant have been used in a former labour.

After her puerperal recovery, Mr Goodman judiciously prescribed for her tonics and other appropriate remedies, and recommended her to the sea-side for the benefit of bathing. Her health was greatly improved, and perhaps the progress of the mollities ossium was temporarily arrested. The disease again returned, and produced effects on the pelvis, during her pregnancy, which rendered necessary the Cæsarean section for her delivery.

Many circumstances existed in this case which favoured its propitious termination. Her calm and tranquil state of mind, and the high degree of moral courage she had, were very advantageous.

An early rupture of the membranes, in protracted labours, especially if the pains are strong, is always to be deplored ; but, most fortunately, this did not happen here very long before the performance of the operation. The water was not suddenly and completely discharged at once, but dribbled away. The pains were also very feeble, until a very short time before my visit. The conjoined effects of these were doubtless favourable, and prevented injurious pressure on the soft parts. The bowels were freely evacuated during her labour. By the aid of the stethoscope the incision was made in a direction to avoid cutting into the placenta, which is very important.

When the placenta is cut upon or into, partial irregular contraction of the uterus happens, and through such an accident the infant may be lost, as I have already stated ; but besides this, the tissue of the uterus is likely to suffer from the force required to extricate it (the infant) from the spasmodic grasp of this organ. Besides, there may be a greater risk of hæmorrhage when the placenta is prematurely disrupted or separated.

The operation was timely performed in this case. There happened several important contingent circumstances, which I shall briefly advert to. The abdominal parietes were so attenuated as only to allow a very slender hold to be taken by sutures, and were quite unequal to resist the pressure they were subjected to. · By the force of the cough, etc., this weak structure was torn through, and the edges being thereby set at liberty, retracted on each side to a considerable extent, and exposed the bowels fully seven to eight inches in one direction by three to five in the other. Notwithstanding this serious accident, the constitutional disturbance was only trifling in degree and of short duration.

The changes which successively took place on the exposed surface of the bowels, were truly astonishing. A thin transparent effusion of lymph was first seen laid over the peritoneal coat of the intestines, which entered a little into the depressions formed between their convolutions. This thin gelatinous material gradually became thicker and more opaque,—evidently the second step towards cicatrisation. During this wonderful process—for its effects were truly wonderful—innumerable vessels were seen, destined to carry on this great work of reparation. As this went on, there was a progressive and perceptible diminution in the size of the surface ; and when completed, there was cicatrix to be seen very little different from one which is formed after the healing of a wound whose edges have been kept in juxtaposition.

Symptoms of strangulation appeared, for the relief of which several expedients were adopted ; the protruded portion of the bowel was ineffectually punctured. Nature, however, stepped in, and immediately the symptoms were relieved by the formation of an opening through which a great quantity of fæculent matter and flatus was discharged. This aperture, as is mentioned in the reports, continued throughout the case. Although this disaster protracted the patient's recovery, there is no doubt it had, at the time it happened, a most salutary effect. During the whole period of the case the bowels were strictly attended to ; and there is no doubt their ready obedience to our measures (chiefly enemata) considerably contributed to her recovery.

The reparative process which happened in this case, and the decidedly conservative constitutional power which this woman had, prove beyond dispute that the opinion expressed by my friend Dr. West (*London Medical Gazette*, No. 1210, February 1851, p. 245) is not infallibly true, and therefore ought not to influence us and deter us from the performance of the Cæsarean section. The same restorative power was observed in the other successful case, which is already before the profession.

As it was important to preserve the infant, I strenuously urged Mr. Sankey to obtain a wet-nurse ; and no time was lost in obtaining one. The infant continued to thrive, and lived rather more than seven months. Her death was occasioned by an hydrocephaloid disease—the consequence of exhaustion from diarrhœa.

SEQUEL. Mrs. Sankey became again pregnant ; but, as I was not consulted in her case, I can only give the account published by her medical attendant (see *British Record*, page 14). It is stated, "information was received on the 25th of September, that Mrs. Sankey was again pregnant : at this time the catamenial flow had ceased for two months, but there was no enlargement of the mammæ or change in the areola of the nipples ; no morning sickness was experienced, and there existed no perceptible change in the desires of the stomach, or in the organs of sensation ; still there was a progressive increase in the size of the abdomen, and a feeling on the part of the patient that she was decidedly pregnant.

"Having, at length, determined upon the course to be pursued, we directed, at first, drachm doses of secale cornut. to be administered daily, and afterwards twenty grains of the same, at more frequent intervals. On the 28th of September, we commenced the administration of the infus. sabinæ, in gradually increasing doses, beginning with six grains ; this was continued until the 12th of October, when half-drachm doses were administered, combined with the same quan-

tity of secale cornut. ter in die.   These measures, with the pil. aloes
c. myrrh as an aperient, formed the method of treatment until the
29th of October, at which time Mrs. Sankey, experiencing no change
in any respect, entreated us to desist from any further attempt.   In
consequence of our inability to detect any symptom, by which to determine that the desired action of the remedies employed had taken
place, we abstained from the further administration of remedial
agents, with the exception of the pil. aloes c. myrrh, as an occasional
aperient.   After this period, our patient remained in tolerable health
and spirits, and continued as free from the occurrence of uterine
pains, weight, or unpleasant feeling, as since the commencement of
the treatment, until the morning of December 7th, which was more
than a full month after the discontinuance of these measures.   On
this day, being summoned to attend, I discovered that during the
night Mrs. Sankey had aborted a fœtus of about two months growth,
at which both the patient and myself were well pleased ; and, with
the exception of some vomiting, she continued to progress favourably
for two or three days.   The placenta, however, was delayed ; and, although no hæmorrhage of any moment occurred, anxiety was experienced on this account ; it was detected protruding from the os
uteri, from which it was impossible to remove it.   Ordered sec. corn.,
two drachms aq. fervent., three ounces ; ft. infusum stat. sumendus ;
and, for the sickness, a saline mixture was ordered to be taken during
effervescence.   The secale cornutum was repeated on the following
day, but during the interval many attempts were made, both by
manipulation and instruments, to remove the placenta, which was
now lying impacted in the brim of the pelvis.   On the third day I
was enabled sufficiently to lay hold of it, so as, by very strained
exertion, between two fingers used as forceps with the assistance of
pressure on the abdomen, to succeed in extracting it entire.   This
desirable accomplishment produced considerable satisfaction ; for Mrs.
Sankey was already beginning to suffer from the fœtid and decom-
posing condition of the retained placenta.   Some febrile action was
now observed in the system, and even typhoid symptoms were, in
some measure, anticipated ; and, after the removal of the placenta,
the patient complained of slight tenderness in the region of the old
wound.   The hæmorrhage was so slight, that it merely saturated
three napkins ; the vomiting increased, and a mustard poultice was
applied to the epigastrium.   Other remedies were also employed, but
the patient gradually sunk, exhausted by continual vomiting, and
the shock of parturition.   She died on the 12th of December ; and,
on the evening of the following day, we made a *post mortem examination* of the body."

   " Post Mortem Examination.   On inspecting the body an orifice,
the size of a pin point, was discovered in the situation of the original
wound, and the linen around it was moistened by about six drops of
slightly coloured serous fluid.   On opening the abdomen, a general
glueing and matting together of the arch of the colon and omentum
to the adjacent intestines (in an area of the extent of eight or nine
inches) and to the cicatrised skin of the abdomen, was observed ;
which, as will be remembered, was developed from, and healed upon,
the exposed peritoneal covering of these viscera.   Much flatulent
distention of the colon existed, and it was fully proved, that no
Cœsarean section could have been again performed."

   " The agglutination of the parts, through which the incision must have penetrated, rendered the performance utterly impossible. It would have been necessary (as it was in simply opening the body after death) to have dissected the skin from the subjacent omentum; and the dissection must have been continued, until the whole of the skin under this covering had been completely separated from its adhesions to the smaller intestines; and they, also, would have required separating from each other, before the uterus could have been exposed. Fatal as the case had proved, we could not avoid a feeling of satisfaction that the measures adopted had been directed towards the induction of abortion, instead of reserving the mother for an operation, which would have proved fatal in the very hour of performance. The gall bladder and duodenum were distended with black bile; and the uterus was empty, and considerably congested at its fundus. The cicatrix of the original incision into the uterus was well defined, and there was no adhesion of the fundus to any adjoining viscera. There were no other decided marks of inflammatory action." The opening into the cavity of the pelvis, instead of presenting its proper oval form, had assumed a tripartite or trilobed character.*

It is further stated that "a perpendicular section of the pelvis, showing the projection of the sacrum ossa ilii, and the cavity of the vagina, etc., was about three inches in its perpendicular axis." " From the pubes to the margin of the ribs seven inches and three-quarters, to the point of the sternum only nine inches." The pubis and conjoined ossa ilii" were " seen projecting inwards and backwards, and thus diminishing also the vaginal cavity" at the outlet. " The tuberosities of the ischium (ischia) joined at the centre. The anterior fissure between these bones was only half an inch in diameter, the posterior opening was laterally two inches, and antero-posteriorly two inches and three-quarters diameter."

Some of the above quotations were given as explanatory of three small figures; but as they are intended to point out some measurements, I have inserted them.

The aforesaid remarks are solely quoted for the purpose of making the interesting case of Mrs. Sankey complete, and not to indicate an approval of the course adopted.

The agglutination and matting together of some of the abdominal viscera which took place, is attributable to the yielding of the edges of the wound and the protrusion of part of the intestines.

The adherent state of the abdominal viscera is amply sufficient to arrest gestation and consequently lead to abortion. Therefore, there is little doubt if the case had been left to Nature the ovum would have been most assuredly expelled without artificial interference.

CASE (Tab.) 51 (*Unsuccessful*). The following case has been most kindly and liberally given to me by James Braid, Esq., M.R.C.S.Ed., C.M.W.S., etc., for the purpose of publication :—

" My dear Sir,—I beg to hand you the following brief particulars of the case of Cæsarean section in which I operated in 1847. So far as it goes, it fully justifies the doctrine you so ably and properly advocate :—

" About one o'clock P.M., on the 15th June 1847, I was requested to go to Wilmslow, in Cheshire, to perform the Cæsarean

---

* See Figure 5th.

section in the case of a poor woman named Mrs. Toft, who had been in labour since early on the morning of the 12th—that was three days and a half—and for whom the surgeons in attendance considered there was no hope of relief otherwise than by such operation. I consequently started by the first railway train, accompanied by my son, and arrived at the house of the patient by half-past two o'clock.

"The patient was said to be about 30 years of age, and had been married twenty-one months. She became pregnant shortly after marriage, but aborted at the third month. On the present occasion she had arrived at the full term of utero-gestation before calling for professional aid, which, indeed, she did only after labour had commenced, which was early on the morning of the 12th. Mr. Mayson, surgeon, of Wilmslow, had attended her alone, from Saturday morning till Monday morning, when he had Mr. Dean, surgeon, of the same place, associated with him, who continued his attendance along with Mr. Mayson up to the period when Mr. Dean came to request my aid.

"The patient had always been of a feeble constitution, with fair complexion; but now she was excessively pale and exhausted, and was much disfigured by a large bronchocele. Her pulse was very rapid and feeble. On examination, the first object which attracted attention was the arm of a well developed child protruding from the vagina, proving it to be a case of shoulder presentation. The bones of the outlet of the pelvis were so crushed together, that there was scarcely room for one finger to pass by the side of the protruding arm, so as to make an examination. The arm being pushed up, I ascertained that the rami of the pubes were so closely approximated that a finger placed edgeways could not reach the symphysis pubis; and the tubera ischii were only about an inch apart, for there was no point where two fingers, placed side by side, could pass when placed transversely; indeed, owing to the close approximation of the rami pubis, tubera ischii, and os coccygis, there was barely room sufficient to permit two fingers to pass the outlet of the pelvis in the antero-posterior direction. Owing to the shallowness of the pelvis, however, which must have been originally of small dimensions, I was the more readily enabled to reach and determine the dimensions of the brim. I ascertained that there was not as much available space in the antero-posterior direction as to permit the points of two fingers laid side by side to pass the brim of the pelvis,* excepting about half an inch, exactly opposite the symphysis pubis, and there the fingers had barely room to pass. Beyond this, on either side, there appeared to be very little more than an inch of available space in the antero-posterior direction. The transverse diameter might exceed three inches; but then it was a crescentic form, which, of course, made it completely unavailable for delivery.

"My son having also made an examination of the patient, and made a similar estimate of the relative position of the bones of the pelvis at the brim and at the outlet, which were, moreover, firm and unyielding, we had no difficulty, in consultation with the other two surgeons, Mr. Mayson and Mr. Dean, in arriving at the conclusion that the woman must die undelivered if we did not instantly resort to the Cœsarean section. With such deformity as existed here in the pelvic bones, it must have been all but impossible to have broken down and extracted the fully developed child (which from the protruding

---

* See Figure 6th.

arm this evidently was), even in a vigorous patient; but in a feeble woman like the one in question, exhausted to the last degree by the length of time she had been in labour, and the violence and acute suffering which she experienced from the pains, even up to the period when we were with her, it would have been perfectly futile and absurd to have made any attempt of the sort.

" The extreme violence and excruciating agony which the patient was suffering from the pains, rendered it the more desirable that the operation should not be unnecessarily delayed ; and we therefore stated our views of the whole bearing of the case fully and fairly to the friends, and obtained their consent, and subsequently the patient's also, when I proceeded to perform the operation in the usual manner at three o'clock. I deem it quite unnecessary to occupy your time by giving any details of the operation ; for, although a formidable and a most important one, and one which ought only to be performed from the necessity of the case, still, *quasi* a surgical operation, it involves comparatively little difficulty to those well acquainted with the anatomy of the parts and are in the frequent habit of operating. A very few minutes sufficed to make the necessary incisions and to extract the child, the placenta, and the coagula found in the uterus. All this—the stitching, dressing, and replacing the patient in bed— did not exceed ten minutes ; and the whole pain sustained by the patient in consequence of the operation did not appear much to exceed a single pain, such as she had in our presence from the throes of nature before we proposed the operation to her.

"The infant was large and well developed, but was dead, obviously from previous detachment of the placenta, for it was found quite detached, and surrounded by coagula, which at once accounted for the exsanguine appearance of the mother, as well as for the death of the child. There had been very little coloured discharge *per vaginam*, the egress having been completely closed by the shoulder of the child being impacted into the brim of the pelvis. Very little blood was lost by the incisions made during the operation, and very little passed *per vaginam* subsequently. After the operation the patient seemed to suffer no more pain, but she passed quietly away, from exhaustion, five hours and a half after the operation.

"On the 17th I went over, accompanied by my son and another medical friend, for the purpose of having a post-mortem examination. Mr. Dean was also with us. We had almost been too late, as the company had assembled before our arrival for the purpose of interring the body. They consented to postpone it a very short time to allow us to make an inspection, but we were necessarily compelled to be very circumspect, as we were closely watched, and were thus prevented the opportunity of possessing ourselves of the pelvis. However, I had used the precaution of taking some plaster of Paris with us, and thus we were enabled to take an accurate model of the inlet of the pelvis. From this it was satisfactory to find that the estimate made of the brim of the pelvis, previous to undertaking the operation, had been very correct, as the following measurements of the cast prove :—About an inch immediately opposite the symphysis pubis; the diameter of the brim of the pelvis, from the symphysis pubis to the lumbar vertebræ, was one inch and three-eighths, and beyond that, on the left side, it abruptly diminished to nine-eighths of an inch ; and from that to half an inch and nothing ; and on the right side to an inch and a quarter to an inch, and from that to the segment of a small circle. The transverse diameter, from right to left, was three inches and a half, but of this there was not more than two inches which would admit a ball to pass where it exceeded an inch in diameter. But, as already stated, the brim had assumed a crescentic form, so that when two straight parallel lines were drawn across the pelvis, they only showed two inches by one inch as the largest available space. Under these circumstances, therefore, it is quite obvious that delivery, by mutilation of the infant, could not have been undertaken with any hope of success at any stage of the labour, however vigorous the patient might have been; how much less so then, with such a constitution as we had here to encounter, and with a shoulder presentation, too, the cavity of the pelvis was so small as not to admit a body greater than a lemon. At the left side and anterior part of the fundus uteri the walls of the uterus were fully an inch and a half in thickness, whilst a considerable portion on the posterior and right side was attenuated in an extreme degree; so that from this circumstance, and the violent and cutting character of the pains witnessed by us, had she been left a short time longer undelivered, in all probability rupture of the uterus and death would have been the result. Very little blood had escaped *per vaginam* subsequent to the operation, and there was only a small clot found within the cavity of the uterus.

"Here, then, is a case which I think fully justifies the Cæsarean section; for no medical man had been consulted until the woman was in labour at the full term of utero-gestation, and with physical attributes which rendered it impossible for her to be delivered in any other manner than by the Cæsarean section. The only cause of regret is that this had not been undertaken immediately after labour commenced; for in that case there is every reason to believe that the life of the infant would have been spared, with a tolerable chance of safety for the mother also.

"This alternative had been proposed to the patient before I was sent for, but she obstinately held out against submitting to any such operation. I consider it but an act of justice to Mr. Dean and Mr. Mayson to record this fact; and it took some management on my own part to obtain her consent at last. Although the operation failed to save the life of mother or child, still it relieved her of suffering for the last five hours and a half of her life, and her friends the pain of hearing her piercing screams, and witnessing the agonising throes which accompanied the unavailing efforts of nature to relieve her from her perilous condition.

"You can please append any remarks to this case which your experience in such cases may suggest to you.

"Believe me, my dear sir,
"yours very faithfully,
"JAMES BRAID.

"Arlington House,   "Dr. Radford, etc., etc.,
       "May 8th, 1851.   Manchester."

DR. RADFORD'S REMARKS.—Malacosteon doubtless was the disease which caused the distortion of the pelvis of this poor creature; there are no data whereby to judge when its ravages on the bones commenced. Some of the contingent circumstances which happened clearly prove the truth of those statements I made a short time ago (vide *London Medical Gazette* for April 4th, 1851, vol. 47, p. 583).

It was her first labour, and we have no evidence to show that any symptoms existed, either before or during her pregnancy, to induce her to place herself under medical treatment. The obstetrician was completely ignorant of the physical and organic condition of the pelvis until after labour had began. It is then indisputably true that no other operation but the Cæsarean could possibly or safely be performed for her delivery. The great mischief of procrastinating the operation is emphatically proved by the result. Several serious evils arising from protracted labour are noticed by Mr. Braid. The death of the infant was undoubtedly produced by it, and most likely that of the mother. The internal flooding, the complete separation of the placenta, and the attenuated state of one portion of the structure of the uterus, which no doubt would have ended in its rupture, are solely to be attributed to delay.

In Cases 30 and 41 (Tab.), I have mentioned that violent irregular uterine contraction happened during the extractions of the infant, which, I stated, depended on the partial or complete detachment of the placenta ; in the foregoing case, however, nothing of the kind took place, although this organ was lying loose in the uterus. Did the internal bleeding (which was so great as to bleach the general surface) act on the uterine tissue, and so influence its contractility ? Was the absence of this spasm (when its supposed cause was present) owing to the extreme degree of attenuation of the uterine tissue ?

CASE (Tab.) 53 (*Successful*). The subject of this case—Mary, wife of William Haigh—resides at Flats Fold, a mile from Ashton-under-Lyne, and about eight miles from Manchester. On my arrival, at half-past three o'clock P.M., I called upon Mr. Cluley, who accom · panied me to the case, and, with the greatest courtesy and candour, gave me, as we passed along, the following particulars :—She had felt slight pains, according to the account of the friends, about a week ; but Mr. Cluley thought that true parturient pains had only existed about three days, and which were so slight as not to require his interference. On this day (Sunday, May 20th, 1849), at nine o'clock, he was again called, and although the pains were still trifling, he made an examination *per vaginam*, but was unable to feel either the os uteri or the presentation ; he therefore had her taken out of bed and placed on the lap of a female friend, and again repeated his inquiry. The head of the infant was now felt, and the os uteri found dilated to the size of a half-crown piece. In this manœuvre he unintentionally ruptured the membranes. The pelvis, he mentioned, was considerably contracted.

I found her lying on the right side. Pulse 120; tongue clean and moist ; her countenance tranquil, but a little flushed. Her bowels had been freely and fully moved this morning, and she had also freely and duly urinated : she was helplessly fixed on her side, and, when requested to turn, she remarked she suffered very great pain when she made an attempt to do so, or was by another person turned on the back. The pelvis was very considerably altered from its natural shape ; its sides were flatter, and the posterior division of the ilia, especially on the left side, projected backwards, and the upper portion of the sacrum and the lower lumbar vertebræ had sunk in an inward and downward direction, so that a great concavity was perceived here. The uterus inclined rather to the right side, and stood considerably more forward than usual, although it had not resumed the retort form to the same degree as I have witnessed in former cases ; its tissue felt soft and compressible. The fundus or upper division of the organ was fluctuant, and rounder in shape than it generally is after the discharge of the liquor amnii, which led me to conclude that a great portion of this fluid still remained. This opinion was corroborated when I attempted to ascertain the position of the infant; for at the lower or cervical portion of the uterus, from whence it was assumed the fluid had escaped, the projections of its body could only be felt.

By a vaginal examination, I found the lower aperture of the pelvis very considerably diminished by the close approximation of the rami of the ischia and pubes, which nearly destroyed the arch, and by their jutting forward there remained only a narrow slit, which would not admit the point of a finger. In the transverse diameter, two fingers could only be just placed between the tubera ischii ; the antero-posterior diameter was also much shortened by the coccyx and the lower part of the sacrum being considerably incurvated. This great diminution in the outlet rendered it difficult to measure the brim, so that it was necessary to carry the hand very far backwards to accomplish it. Its figure was tripartite, or composed of three divisions. This alteration in the brim was occasioned by the falling downwards and forwards of the upper part of the sacrum and the lower lumbar vertebræ, which inclined a little more to the left side, and by the body of the ossa pubis and ischii being forced backwards and inwards, and by the jutting forwards of the symphysis and rami of the pubes.* The measurement of the widest part of the conjugate diameter, in the two lateral divisions, did not exceed an inch and a half; I could only place two fingers, one lying a little over the other. The anterior division was not more than half an inch in its widest part, as it would scarcely admit one finger edge-ways. The length of this narrow opening is not relatively available in practice. In the transverse diameter of the brim I could just place three fingers parallel with each other. The external genitals were free from tumefaction, and the vaginal lining was moist, and of a natural temperature. Whilst lying on her side, I was unable to feel either the os uteri or the presenting part of the infant; but on placing her on her back (which occasioned her great pain), the os was felt to be dilated to rather more than the size of a shilling. She had not felt the movement of the infant since the morning, but, by the stethoscope I satisfactorily heard the pulsation of its heart, which fact Mr. Cluley afterwards corroborated.

With my opinion as to the position the Cæsarean section ought to take in obstetrics, I at once concluded that it was the only operation that was justifiable, and indeed capable of giving the best chance of life to both mother and infant. Mr. Cluley most cordially acquiesced in this opinion. We now informed her husband of the nature of the case, and the means to be adopted. He answered, " if nothing else would save her, he willingly submitted to any plan we considered right." When a similar proposition was made to the poor woman, she received it with the greatest resignation ; it was unaccompanied by either mental or physical disturbance. At Mr.

---

* See Figure 7th.

Cluley's request, Dr. Lees, Messrs. Hunt, Gibbons, Galt, and Brewster were present at the operation. Before the incision was made, I was anxious, as far as possible, to ascertain where the placenta was located, and I therefore placed my ear over the left division of the uterus. From the negative evidence, I concluded that it was not fixed on this side of that organ. Mr. Cluley adopted the same plan, but thought he heard the placental *soufflet.* I again applied my ear —still heard nothing. Dr. Lees tried, and considered the sound to arise from the friction of the ear on an interposed piece of linen. Mr. Cluley, after a second trial, agreed in my opinion. I therefore suggested the left side of the linea alba as the proper situation to make the incision. I now raised the fundus uteri, and Mr. Cluley divided the abdominal integuments on the left side of the umbilicus to about six inches in extent, from which very little blood was lost. An opening now was made into the uterus by a scalpel, which was further extended upwards and downwards by the probe-pointed bistoury. At this stage some little bleeding took place from the divided sinuses, and there was also a considerable discharge of liquor amnii. I now, as quickly as possible, introduced one hand into the uterus, over the infant's hip, and fixed the fingers under the flexed thigh in the groin, and having placed the other hand on the opposite of its breech, I extracted it vigorously alive. During this manœuvre, the uterus strongly and regularly contracted. The funis was now tied and divided by one of the gentlemen present. Afterwards, I seized the funis with one hand, and with the other readily detached and brought away the placenta, which was fixed on the right latero-posterier surface of the uterus. There was some blood discharged ; but not more than frequently happens after ordinary or natural labour. Several convolutions of intestines, with a portion of omentum, now protruded, which had up to this time been supported and effectually restrained under the abdominal parietes, but they were readily returned. I carried my finger round the wound to ascertain if any portion of these viscera had descended into the uterus. The integuments were brought into proximity, and held together for a short time by a hand placed on each side ; and, as there was no further discharge of blood, ligatures were inserted at an inch distance from each other. Mr. Cluley used a long needle with a scalpel-like handle for this purpose, which admirably answered : it is much superior to those in ordinary use. Straps of adhesive plaster were laid across the wound, and on each side a compress of lint was placed, and over all a bandage, just tight enough to give a firm support. During the whole time her mind was calm; she never even uttered a complaint. She remarked that her sufferings during the operation had been much less than what she had endured previously to it. Pulse from 80 to 90 in the minute. Tinct. opii ℥iss administered.

Half-past seven. Pulse 100 to 120; dozing ; there was no hæmorrhage or vomiting ; had taken some gruel. Ordered mucilaginous beverages and farinaceous diet. At a later hour the same evening, Mr. Cluley saw her, and found a little abdominal uneasiness. She had slept and had a lochial discharge.

May 21st, Monday, half-past two P.M. Pulse 130; tongue moist ; face less flushed ; abdomen tympanitic and slightly painful ; fresh and plentiful lochia; bowels not moved ; five ounces of water drawn by catheter; continue mucilaginous drinks, etc. An enema of warm water to be administered in the morning.

23rd, Tuesday, half-past nine A.M. Mr. Cluley had ordered forty drops of tinct. opii to be taken at bedtime. She had several times vomited a dark-coloured fluid during the night, and she still continues to do so; pulse 120; abdomen tympanitic, but not tender; tongue slightly furred; lochia natural; bowels still unmoved. After loosening the bandage, there was a discharge of sanious matter. Ordered an enema with ol. ricini ʒj; spt. terebinth. ʒij, etc. To take ext. col. co. gr. x; hyd. chlorid. gr. ij.

23rd, Wednesday, half-past nine A.M. Hiccough has been troublesome; has bilious vomiting; tongue brownish; pulse 120; has a burning sensation in the throat, and the side of her mouth is excoriated; she says she tastes the turpentine which was given in the enema; bowels not moved. Ordered sodæ sub borat. ʒij; aq. destillat. ʒiij; mist. acaciæ ʒiij; capt. ʒj tertiis horis. Gumwater to drink. To have an enema with three ounces of ox-gall and a pint of water.

24th, Thursday, half-past nine A.M. Symptoms continue the same; but the tongue is slightly aphthous; two enemata were administered, which produced two small scybalous stools; wound much lessened in size, but its edges are flabby and have not united; ligatures still firm. To continue the same plan; to have the ox-gall enema repeated.

25th, Friday, half-past nine A.M. All the symptoms better; has had free alvine evacuation. The integuments over the sacrum are inflamed and excoriated, and have a tendency to slough. To continue the same means. Ordered warm water enema. The parts over the sacrum to be dressed with collodion; warm water to be injected *per vaginam* into the uterus.

26th, Saturday, half-past nine A.M. Tongue red and clean; bowels twice freely opened; has vomited several times since yesterday; wound granulating and looking well. To continue the same plan.

27th, Sunday, nine A.M. Had suffered from occasional deafness and tinnitus aurium yesterday. This morning she is not so well. Pulse 125 and tremulous; the tinnitus aurium and deafness still continue; has numbness of one arm and leg; the bowels not moved. To take a little milk, to have a warm water enema administered, and afterwards one of milk. To take ammon. sesquicarb. if required.

28th, Monday, half-past nine A.M. Yesterday, not so well; had delirious rambling. Pulse from 120 to 130; great restlessness and tossing about; was low in spirits; seemed much weaker; the bowels were moved; has taken the ammonia. She is much better this morning, and has had some sleep. The wound was patulous, and from it a dark-coloured and fetid fluid escaped. To continue milk diet; warm water to be thrown *per vaginam* into the uterus.

29th, Tuesday, half-past nine A.M. All the symptoms are better; the wound is filling up by granulation; one ligature came away. The bandage was wet, from the water which had been injected *per vaginam* into the uterus escaping through the wound. Slough over the sacrum came away, and the sores are looking well. Collodion to be again applied; to have a warm water enema first, and afterwards one containing ox-gall, if required.

From the above date up to June 7th, nothing occurred in the character of the symptoms to require particular comment. She continued progressively to improve. The wound gradually filled up by granulation, and is at this time nearly healed. The fistulous opening, through which the water, which had been injected *per vaginam* into the uterus, had escaped, is now completely obliterated. The sores over the back part of the sacrum, and on the nates, are also quite well.

During this period the diet chiefly consisted of milk ; but towards the end of it animal food was allowed once a day. The mucilaginous mixture, with sodæ sub-boras, was the only medicine which she took, except the gum-water. When the bowels required relief, an enema of warm water was first administered, and, if necessary, this was followed by one containing ox-gall.

The collodion was continued as a dressing to the raw surfaces behind, until the latter part of the time, when pads of cotton, with a mild unguent, were substituted. During my absence from Manchester, I received favourable reports of the patient from Mr. Gibbon, under whose professional care she was placed, in consequence of Mr. Cluley's severe illness. In his last letter, dated June 18th, he says : "The wound is very healthy, but not quite healed."

June 26th, Tuesday. I visited her along with Mr. Cluley, and found her down stairs, and looking very well ; she remarked she was in excellent health. On removing the dressings, we found two or three spots of exuberant granulations, which only required the application of argent nitras and a little dry lint.

July 15th, Sunday. I called upon Mrs. Haigh. She was looking extremely well, and in excellent spirits. She observed she was better ; and could walk with more ease to herself than she could have done for a long time before the operation ; the wound was quite healed.

It was a great object with us, that the infant's life should be preserved. We, therefore, strenuously recommended a wet-nurse ; and, if one could not be obtained, then that it should be supplied with asses' milk ; but from unavoidable circumstances, neither were procured until its life was placed in great danger. All those mischiefs consequent upon dry-nursing appeared : such as bowel affections, a threating of marasmus, and convulsions. At length, a nurse was obtained, after which the infant improved, and on this day is quite well.

Before I proceed further, I take this opportunity of mentioning, the surgical part of the operation was most skilfully and dexterously performed by Mr. Cluley ; and his punctual, assiduous, and unremitting attention to the patient, are highly honourable to him. To him I am personally indebted, and return him my sincere thanks for his uniform great kindness and courtesy.

REMARKS. Mary Haigh was occupied before her marriage as a domestic servant, and was then strong, and capable of undergoing great exertion. She is of a sanguineo-lymphatic temperament ; her skin fair, with a red blush on the cheeks ; her hair of an auburn or reddish-brown colour ; the tint of her eyes is rather peculiar, being of a brownish-grey, and they have an animated expression. Her father is now living and very healthy. Her mother has been dead many years ; and, most likely, her death was occasioned by some chronic disease of the vertebræ, as I understood she was afflicted with abscess in the back.

Our patient is 31 years of age, and has been married nearly nine. During this period she has had five children. The labours of the first four were natural and quick ; the last of this number happened three years ago, and was so rapid that the infant was born before the obstetrician arrived. After the birth of the second, she was rather more delicate, and suffered a little from indigestion ; and

about five or six years since, first complained of slight rheumatic
pains about her hips. Two years since she was confined to bed for
a short time, by pains about the pelvis; but she gradually recovered,
and afterwards was able to walk about tolerably well. Her general
health remained the same up to the period of her last pregnancy.
She was now observed to limp a little when she walked, and to be
less in height.

During her gestation her progression was more difficult, and her
gait more waddling. She also complained more of pelvic pains, and
the diminution in her stature now evidently increased. Mollities ossium, the disease under which she suffered, usually commences during
pregnancy, and generally becomes suspended in the interval, returning in an aggravated form in each successive pregnancy, until its
ravages have completely destroyed the form of the pelvis. In this
case, however, it did not exactly pursue this course. There is no
doubt there existed a strong predisposition to the disease—most
likely hereditary; and, probably, the disease began at the latter part
of the second pregnancy; but, evidently, no great, if any mischief,
was done to the pelvis at this time, or for a long time after this
period, as the third and fourth labours were so rapidly and easily
terminated. The rapidity of its progress is remarkable ; for there is
little doubt that the great degree of distortion took place immediately
before and during the last pregnancy. Sometimes in this disease
the bones are so soft that they yield when the hand is introduced to
make an examination. This happened here, as Mr. Cluley thought
he felt a giving way of the bones when he examined the pelvis.

Opium is generally given after great operations, to lessen the shock
on the nervous system; but, in the present instance, we had no evidence that such an effect existed, and therefore, on this account, the
drug might have been omitted. A second dose was administered by
Mr. Cluley, to which he attributed the vomiting which afterwards
occurred. He considered that it had produced an effect similar to
that which follows a debauch. It most likely constipated the bowels ;
but there is no doubt that this was chiefly caused by the bowel being
compressed between the bulky uterus and the projection of the lower
lumbar vertebræ and promontory of the sacrum. The garrulous de-
lirium, the convulsive twitchings, and tinnitus aurium, etc., were
considered by Mr. Cluley to depend on a state requiring more support : we, therefore, agreed to give a milk diet ; and, as its effects
were so satisfactory it was continued to the end.

The negative system of treatment here pursued considerably contributed to the well-doing both of this case and also of the one in
which I was concerned along with Mr. Goodman. I have also observed the same plan most beneficially carried out in the after-treatment of abdominal sections for the extirpation of large ovarian
tumours. There are great objections to the use of purgatives after
these great operations, as the mucous membrane of the bowels is so
readily disturbed : we, therefore, only ordered two doses of pills, and
trusted chiefly to the use of the enemata. The ox-gall enema was
decidedly beneficial.

Rupture of the membranes, and evacuation of the liquor amnii, a
long time before the operation, is always to be deplored ; but, although this accident happened here, yet the great bulk of this fluid
was still retained in the middle and upper portion of the uterus,
which felt fluctuant and round in shape, and which admirably pre-

vented the contraction of this organ, and so thereby lessened the chance of mischievous pressure on the maternal structures, and also contributed to the safety of the infant, and rendered its extraction more easy. The length of the uterine wound was also thereby diminished, in a degree proportional to the difference in the measurement of the uterine tissue, when distended by the contained fluid, and after its evacuation, when shortened by contraction.

In the present case, happily, the water was not evacuated until a short time before the operation, and then only very partially; the pains were also fortunately so slight, that no injurious pressure was made.

SEQUEL. The following particulars of this highly valuable case will be especially interesting to most of my obstetric readers :—

Mary Haigh lived rather more than four years after she had recovered from the performance of the Cæsarean section, during which time she grew less in stature, and had great pain and difficulty in turning herself in bed. She was carried up and down stairs, and, as she was unable to move about, she was constantly confined to a sitting position. She was quite unequal to dress and undress herself. She suffered from pains about the pelvis. She, nevertheless, took great interest in, and partially attended to, her domestic duties until about twelve months before her death.

Her appetite continued good until a few months before her death, during which time she ate very little and had great loathing of her food, and had nausea. Her bowels were generally constipated, and she experienced great difficulty in voiding her stools. She had occasionally a slight cough as from cold. Menstruation continued regular nearly to the end of life. She gradually lost flesh and declined in power. She died on the second day of June, 1853.

POST-MORTEM EXAMINATION. Her body was greatly emaciated. The point of the sternum approximated very nearly to the pubes which jutted upwards ; the spine was very short, and incurvated outwards. The lower limbs were very thin ; but they were not shortened in length. On opening the abdomen the parietes were found very thin and attenuated. The viscera were generally pale, but every organ appeared healthy. The bladder was nearly empty, and was situated over the brim of the pelvis. The uterus was of the usual size, and rested over the brim of the pelvis. There was only a single band of lymph not thicker than a thread, passing from the anterior surface of this organ to the peritoneum. The uterine tissue was uniform in appearance, and there was not the slightest evidence to shew the site of the incision.

Pelvis. The superior or false pelvis was considerably altered in shape and lessened, and, indeed, it is nearly destroyed by the descent of the lower lumbar vertebræ toward the pubes. The expanded alæ ilii are so crushed together as to reduce the concave venters to deep narrow sulci. The brim is trilobed in shape, there being a very slight slit on each side of the sunken lumbar vertebræ, and one on the anterior slit, which lies between the rami of the pubes which juts out and forwards, and are nearly approximated.*

CASE (Tab.) 58 (*Unsuccessful*). The following case I am enabled to lay before my readers by permission of my esteemed friend, Dr.

---

* See Sketch, Fig. 8th.

Broughton, of Preston. He most liberally consented for me to pub-
lish it, and has furnished me with his copious notes. I shall, as
literally as possible, give the case in Dr. Broughton's own words :—

"Ann, wife of Thomas Kenyon, of Higginson Street, Preston, came
to me as a charity patient, on the 22nd of May, 1851. Her sole occupation was her domestic duties. She was 31 years of age, of a
light complexion, and her eyes were blue. She had suffered from a
cough and felt very weak, and then she complained of pain in the
back and about the hips, and a frequent inability to pass her water,
except when lying on her belly across the foot of the bed. She
waddled very much in her gait, and used a stick, and stated she had
gradually been getting worse during the last two years. She said
she was afraid she should not be able to walk about long unless she
could obtain some relief. After a very strict inquiry, I could not
ascertain that there was any reason to suppose there was the slightest
hereditary predisposition to the disease (mollities ossium) she was now
suffering from. I examined her very carefully, and found the mischief was chiefly confined to the pelvis.

At this time she felt uncertain in her mind whether she was
pregnant ; but she had some suspicion she was in that state, although
her menstrual periods had been very irregular. I ascertained she
had been pregnant six times before. Five of the labours were quite
natural ; in one a few months previous to the present time she
aborted at the fourth month, and had afterwards suffered a great deal.

I made a vaginal examination, and very carefully endeavoured
to find the uterus, but could not do so. I saw her several times, and
desired her to let me know when she was quite certain about her
pregnancy. On Saturday, July 5th, she called upon me, and stated
she believed she was pregnant and had quickened the day previous.
I again made a vaginal examination, but I was unable to find the
os uteri.

I visited her on several occasions, but without obtaining any
further information ; and, therefore, I took my friend Mr. Haldan
along with me to see her. He examined her, but could not find the
os uteri.

The highly distorted state of the pelvis precluding any chance of
attempting to induce premature labour by any artificial method, we
unhesitatingly decided on the propriety of administering the ergot
of rye. Full doses were at first given three times a day ; but afterwards, each dose was more frequently repeated ; and at last, it was
taken every two hours. Violent sickness occurred, but there was no
uterine action excited, although this practice was continued rather
more than a fortnight. At the expiration of this period, we felt
afraid the fœtus could not pass through the pelvis, and therefore we
decided not to interfere further, but concluded to attend to her general health. For this purpose we gave her cod-liver oil three times a
day. She improved in health and strength, but had the same waddling gait. Her stature, according to her husband's account, was
now upwards of four inches less than it was four years ago. She was
visited from time to time, and her spirits were found uniformly
good, although she was fully aware her child could not be born
naturally. She had been directed to send on the very first indica-
tion of labour, and, on Wednesday, November 12th, at six P.M., her
husband came to inform me. I sent him to request Mr. Haldan to
meet me at the house immediately ; we found she had very slight

pains; and she stated she thought the liq. amnii had escaped; on a vaginal examination, no part either of the child or os uteri could be reached. The soft parts were moist and relaxed. Drs. Radford and Whitehead, of Manchester, having previously been aware of the case, had both most kindly said they would come and assist us; and, well knowing the value and importance of their opinions in such a case, I at once started for Manchester, during which time Mr. Haldan kindly consented to attend to the case.

They both accompanied me, leaving Manchester at half-past two A.M. On our arrival at Preston, we at once proceeded to the house of our patient, and found she had not had very many pains. She was calm and tranquil. Her pains now recurred in regular succession. Drs. Radford and Whitehead, by a very careful vaginal examination, found the whole pelvis so extremely distorted, and could not, after their most strenuous efforts, feel either the os uteri or ascertain the presentation of the child. They were both decidedly of opinion, that it was quite impossible to deliver her by any other means than by the Cæsarean section.

I now sent for my friend Mr. Noble, who, after a careful examination, quite concurred as to the necessity of the Cæsarean section, and being the only available means for her delivery.

By the stethoscope we found the child was alive, but the pulsations of its heart were feeble and frequent, being fully 200 in the minute. The placental *soufflet* was heard over the anterior part of the uterus, and over a space extending to the fundus. No time was lost in commencing the operation. The abdominal parietes were divided by being first pinched up and then pierced by a straight scalpel; and the wound was afterwards enlarged by a button-pointed bistoury on the fingers. The uterus was now brought into view, and was carefully opened. Its tissue was very thin, being very little thicker than strong paper (I would here bear my testimony to the statement of the late Mr. Barlow of Blackburn, and which has been so much discussed). The incision was made directly over the placenta, as we had prognosticated; it was quickly enlarged upwards and downwards by the bistoury on a director, and Dr. Radford most dexterously removed the child and placenta. The uterus rapidly contracted as it were *per saltum.* A large quantity of intestine protruded, but, by the valuable aid of Dr. Whitehead and Mr. Haldan, they were speedily returned and retained. She lost very little blood. The edges of the abdominal wound were now brought together by means of six sutures and long strips of emp. resina, which were supported by a large binder. Tinct. opii ʒj was given to her. She expressed herself as comfortable, and inquired about her child, which now cried lustily. She was under the influence of chloroform during the greatest part of the time; we left her at 7 A.M.

10 A.M. I found her restless; her countenance was anxious, and there was a considerable oozing from the bottom of the wound; her pulse is 132.

12. She is still anxious. I found a large warm cloth on the abdomen, which I removed at once; her pulse was 126. Tinct. opii ʒ ss was administered.

4 P.M. She has vomited three times; she had made water; there was a slight lochial discharge. Her countenance is less anxious, and there is very little oozing from the wound; her pulse is 124.

f

6 P.M. She is better.

9 P.M. She is still better, and free from pain ; she has again passed a little water ; there is no lochial discharge since 4 P.M. Ordered pulv. opii gr. ij, to be taken immediately, and to be repeated at 4 A.M. if necessary.

14th, 9 A.M. She has vomited three times during the night ; she has had little sleep, and has made water freely ; her pulse is 116.

11 A.M. She is easy ; her pulse is 118.

Half-past one. She has vomited once ; she is free from pain ; her pulse is 124. Ordered pulv. opii gr. ij, to be immediately taken.

4 P.M. She was made clean ; her soiled bandages, etc., were removed and replaced by others ; she says she has suffered less than after an ordinary labour. Her respiration is natural ; pulse 124.

Half-past 9 P.M. Her pulse is 128 ; the respiration rather quick ; her cheeks are rather flushed; she has again vomited. Liq. opii sed. gutt. xxv. She took a very little toast, and three tablespoonfuls of almost cold tea.

15th, 10 A.M. She has rested well ; her pulse is 124 ; she has made water three times ; the lochia are free. I now allowed her some weak beef tea, made at my own house.

1 P.M. She is better, easy, and tranquil.

4 P.M. She has had the beef tea ordered this morning, and has slept a little ; her pulse is 124 ; her countenance is placid, and her respiration natural.

10 P.M. Her husband has called, and says she is much worse. Mr. Haldan was then with me, and as I was very unwell, he very kindly saw her alone for me. He found her most anxious and restless ; her pulse was 132 ; her breathing hurried ; vomiting acid and bilious fluid. Mr. Haldan, with the long rectum tube, threw up some warm water, in which some soap was dissolved, but which was at once returned without any fæces. He ordered small doses of potass. bicarb., and a very small quantity of acid. citric., just enough to make it effervesce. She had an excellent night afterwards, and was quite easy at 6 A.M.

16th, 10 A.M. She is quite easy, and had not vomited. Pergat.

3 P.M. On removing the dressings the edges of the wound were seen to gape between the sutures, and at the lowest part the intestines could be perceived. We brought the edges close together with the emp. ladani and emp. resina. The sutures were safe and firm. A clean binder and clean clothes were put on, and she was left quite comfortable.

10 P.M. She has had two loose stools, but is now easy; pulse 128; she says she is better than she has been previously.

17th, 10 A.M. She has been a good deal purged during the night, but is now quite free from pain ; her stools are natural ; the lochia free ; she is less anxious. Ordered mist. cretæ co., with tinct. opii ♏xl, tinct. catechu f. ʒij.

Half-past 3. She is now much better, and free from pain ; her bowels have only been very slightly moved since ten o'clock ; her pulse is 116; she cannot take milk, which makes her sick; she wants a little barley gruel, which is allowed her ; she says "has had a real after pain," and is particularly cheerful ; lochia abundant.

5 P.M. She says she is very comfortable ; pulse 116, and tongue quite clean; she remarked "I think I shall now get through I think." " I have suffered very little indeed."

10 P.M. About this time Mr. Haldan was sent for, as I had been very unwell for the last two days. He arrived at eleven, and found her quite altered in appearance; her pulse small and weak; her face pinched and pale, and in fact she had altogether changed. He was informed she had had a most violent attack of vomiting about eight o'clock, immediately after which she complained of some pain in the belly. On removing the binder, he found the wound open and some parts of the intestines protruding. He sent for me immediately, and on my arrival, about twelve o'clock, we made an attempt to return them, but we could not succeed, as more efficient aid was required than the nurse could afford. We then sent for Mr. Noble, who soon arrived, and we did all we could to replace the protruded bowels and close the wound; we however could not succeed, and as it was quite evident she was sinking, at her request we desisted, and covered them again with a warm moist cloth, and left her, receiving her dying thanks for our attention. She sank at a quarter to six A.M.

At twelve o'clock we went to examine the body and replace the intestines. We found them as we had left them (at one o'clock A.M.), protruding, but much altered in appearance. These viscera were now glued by plastic lymph, and a part of the ilium appeared to be gangrenous, and the omentum adherent to the small intestines. Those bowels which remained in the abdomen looked healthy, with the exception of the ascending colon, which adhered to the fundus of the uterus; on cutting into the uterus it was found healthy and natural. The wound in it was partially closed. The liver was pale, large, and encroached on the chest. There were old bands of adhesion between this organ and the diaphragm, and also between it and the walls of the abdomen. The stomach was distended with flatus, but it was healthy. The heart was large, flabby, and pale. The right lung collapsed, and adherent to the pleura costalis by old bands of adhesion. Its lower part was hepatised and red. The left lung was free, small, and full of frothy mucus. Its lower part was congested at its apex; there was grey deposit; the bladder was healthy. The head was not examined. The brim of the pelvis,* on the right side, was so contracted from the falling forwards of the sacrum, as barely to admit one finger, and anteriorly at the pubes rather less. On the left side there was a little more room; in one part, near the sacro-iliac synchondrosis, it just admitted two fingers in the antero-posterior diameter, but only one in the lateral. In fact it was a notch; the sacrum appeared to have come forwards from the ilium by the elongation of the ligaments. The rectum passed here. In no part could a ball one inch and one-third pass. The ascending rami of the ischia were so closed as to barely admit one finger, and the tuberosities are very nearly approximated. The os coccygis is thrown forwards. Thus the cavity of the pelvis was encroached upon to a very remarkable degree, rendering the introduction of even a very small hand quite impossible, and the longest finger could do little more than reach the promontory of the sacrum. The urethra was drawn upwards and backwards behind the symphysis of the pubis, requiring a very long and curved catheter. This situation of the urethra accounts for the difficulty she had in emptying the bladder. I do not doubt but the uterus was retained above the superior aperture by the state of the bones. Her husband

---

* See Figure 9th.

informed me "she had been growing together during the last two years, and that she gradually got worse and closer together. The child is now alive and quite well, and under a wet nurse."

Dr. Radford's *Remarks*.—In the privilege given to me of making a few remarks on Dr. Broughton's case. I cannot allow the opportunity to pass without expressing my high appreciation of the great humanity and kind attention to the interest of his (a hospital) patient, and for the very ardent desire he showed, not only to bestow on her all the advantage within his reach in Preston, but in travelling sixty miles to obtain further aid. Throughout the entire case his treatment was very judicious, and when he had decided upon the propriety of allowing her to go on to the end of pregnancy, he carefully watched her, and urgently pressed upon her and her husband the necessity of acquainting him as early as possible after labour had commenced. My remarks need only be brief, as I have already, in the preceding observations, treated upon most of the interesting points which are contained in both this and some of the other cases.

This poor woman had been naturally delivered of five full-grown infants—there had been no artificial aid required—and therefore all the pelvic mischief must have been produced after the last labour. The disease had made rapid progress, having commenced about two years before. Its ravages were very great and extensive in the pelvis, involving the brim, cavity, and outlet.

It is quite unnecessary for me to go into the physical character of a pelvis distorted by mollities ossium (and the one belonging to Dr. Broughton's patient was extremely so) to show the difficulties the practitioner has to encounter to ascertain such information as ought to guide his judgment of the case. In this case, Dr. Broughton and his medical friends were all unable, when first consulted, and also afterwards, to find the os uteri; and therefore he most wisely decided not to attempt to induce abortion by any artificial means; if he had done so, he might have produced fatal mischief. The uterus and bladder, in such cases as this, are situated above the brim of the pelvis, and lean very much forwards over the beak-like projection of the approximated rami of the pubes and ischia. Whatever may be said, or even thought, as to the propriety of the induction of premature labour or of abortion in such cases as this, I most positively deny its possibility; to make an attempt would be most unwarrantable (*vide* Observations, *ante*).

This poor creature was greatly afflicted, and her vital powers at a low point, as nearly all those women are who suffer under such a constitution and a local disease.

With the exception of these conditions, her case was one favourable for the operation. Dr. Broughton had taken care that her labour was not too much protracted, and the character of the pains were favourable to the issue—being weak and irregular—so that the head of the infant was not forcibly pressed upon the maternal tissues. It is true the membranes had ruptured at the commencement of the labour, but there had been no mischief done. The employment of the stethoscope had warned us of the position of the placenta, but it was quite impossible to avoid this organ in making the incision, and it was therefore consequently cut upon. By this foreknowledge of the certainty of the placenta being in the way of the incision, I was prepared instantly to pass the right hand and seize one lower extremity of the infant, whilst I passed the left hand downwards so as to embrace its head, and so, by a compound movement, to throw out and raise from the uterus the body of the infant, which lay obliquely, its head being on the brim of the pelvis in the first position. By this rapid extraction I doubt not the infant escaped the grasp of the uterus. This result happened in two of my cases, and has been adverted to in the previous observations. The abdominal parietes were very thin and attenuated, and therefore every care was taken to have them well approximated and supported by ligatures, etc. ; but, notwithstanding all the precautions taken, the parts yielded, and some portions of the bowels protruded, and could not be replaced. This most unfortunate event happened at the end of the fourth day after the operation, and doubtless was produced by the violent attack of vomiting which then took place. Before this occurrence everything promised a favourable issue. She had most certainly vomited on the day of the operation, and again twice on the day after its performance. Chloroform was administered at the commencement of the operation, and she was kept under its influence "during the greatest part of the time" of its performance. Was the vomiting in any degree owing to the chloroform? (see preceding observations, page 25).

Dr. Broughton, in a note December 15th, 1851, says, "The case to me has been a most instructive one, and in all future operations in which a large opening is made in the abdomen, I will use metallic ligatures, and replace at alternate spaces fresh ones at the first dressing; I shall then secure the wound." This suggestion is highly deserving of attentive consideration, and in my opinion its adoption promises to be of great use. It is most important, if possible, to secure the edges of the wound, as there are recorded in the tables other cases in which death resulted in consequence of their giving way. The case of Mrs. Sankey (although she recovered) is an excellent example of the disastrous risks which are produced by such an accident.

EXPLANATION OF PLATES.

Explanation of Figure 1st.

This sketch accurately represents the state and dimensions of the brim of the pelvis belonging to Mary Ashworth (Case 27).

A, B. A line from the sacro-iliac junction to the linea ileo-pectinea opposite on the right side six-eighths of an inch.

C, D. Ditto, ditto, on the left side, five-eighths of an inch.

E, F. A line from the upper edge of the fifth lumbar vertebra, to the linea ileo-pectinea behind the acetabulum, on the right side, three-quarters of an inch.

G, H. Ditto, ditto, on the left side, half an inch.

I, K. Line across the anterior slit, two-eighths of an inch.

Explanation of Figure 2nd.

This outline shows the figure and dimension of the brim of the pelvis belonging to Mary Nixon (Case 30), as accurately as could be ascertained by an examination *per vaginam.*

A, B. A line from the linea ileo-pectinea behind the acetabulum to the most projecting point on the back part of the pelvis, on the right side, nearly one inch.

C, D. Ditto, ditto, on the left side, three-quarters of an inch.

Explanation of Figure 3rd.

This sketch accurately represents the brim of the pelvis belonging to Mary Forrest (Case 41).

A, B. From the upper edge of the fifth lumbar vertebra to the ilium just behind the acetabulum, on the right side, five-eighths of an inch.

C, D. From the same points on the left side, an inch and one-eighth.

E, F. From the inside of symphysis pubis to the upper part of the fifth lumbar vertebra, two inches and six-eighths.

G, H. Across the anterior slit, half an inch.

Explanation of Figure 4th.

The outline in this figure indicates the shape and dimensions of the brim of the pelvis of Mrs. Sankey (Case 49), drawn from the measurements obtained by an accurate examination *per vaginam,* previous to the Cæsarian section.

A, B. A line from the sacro-iliac junction to the iliac pectineal line opposite, on the right side, one inch and a half.

C, D. Ditto, ditto, on the left side, nearly the same.

E, F. A line from the most projecting part behind, to the pubis near the jutting forward of these bones, three-quarters of an inch on right side.

G, H. Ditto, ditto, on the left side, three-quarters of an inch.

I, K. Space between the jutting forward of the pubes, half an inch.

Explanation of Figure 5th.

Sketch of the same (Mrs. Sankey's) pelvis, taken from the diagrams and measurements given in *The British Record,* which were obtained at the *post mortem* examination.

A, B, C, D. Spaces between the acetabula and promontory of the sacrum, on each side of the pelvis, one inch and a quarter.

E, F, G, H. The narrowest measurement, one half to three-quarters of an inch.

It is a misfortune that a more minute and accurate account of the pelvis of this woman was not obtained. It was evidently a little more contracted at her death than it was at the time of the Cæsarean section.

Explanation of Figure 6th.

This sketch shows "a full-sized outline of the brim of the late Mrs. Toft's pelvis, taken from a section of the cast" (Case 51).

Mr. Braid states that the points of two fingers laid side by side could not pass the brim, "excepting about half an inch exactly opposite the symphysis pubis, and there the fingers had barely room to pass. Beyond this, on either side, there was very little more than an inch of available space in the antero-posterior direction."

Explanation of Figure 7th.

The outline in this figure indicates the shape and dimensions of the brim of the pelvis of Mrs. Haigh (Case 53), drawn from the measurements obtained by an accurate vaginal examination previous to the Cæsarean section.

A, B, C, D. The widest part of brim, on each side, an inch and one-eighth.

E, F, G, H. The shortest measurements in the conjugate diameter, seven-eighths of an inch.

I, K. Across the anterior slit, half an inch.

Explanation of Figure 8th.

This sketch shows the extremely contracted state of the brim of the pelvis of the same woman, as found at her death (Case 53, sequel).

A, B. Widest part of brim on the right side, two-eighths of an inch.

C, D. Ditto, ditto, on the left side, rather less.

E, F. Narrowest part on right side, one-eighth of an inch.

G, H. Ditto, ditto, on left side, less.

I, K. Widest space in anterior slit, two eighths of an inch.

The pubes at the commencement of the jutting forward touch each other.

A ball whose diameter is two-eighths of an inch will only just pass through the opening between the projecting forward of the lumbar vertebræ and the ossa pubis.

Explanation of Figure 9th.

This sketch accurately represents the brim of Ann Kenion's pelvis (Case 58).

A, B. A line from the sacro-iliac junction to the linea ileo-pect., just behind the posterior edge of the acetabulum, on the right side, an inch and two-eighths.

C, D. Ditto, ditto, on the left side, an inch and a half.

E, F. A line from behind the anterior part of the acetabulum, to the upper edge of the fifth lumbar vertebra, on the right side, six-eighths of an inch.

G, H. Ditto, ditto, on the left side, an inch and one-eighth.

I, K. Across the middle part of the anterior slit, nearly half an inch.

L, M. Across the widest part, ditto, six-eighths of an inch.

From the line, *L, M,* to the lower portion of the fourth lumbar vertebra, an inch and one-eighth.

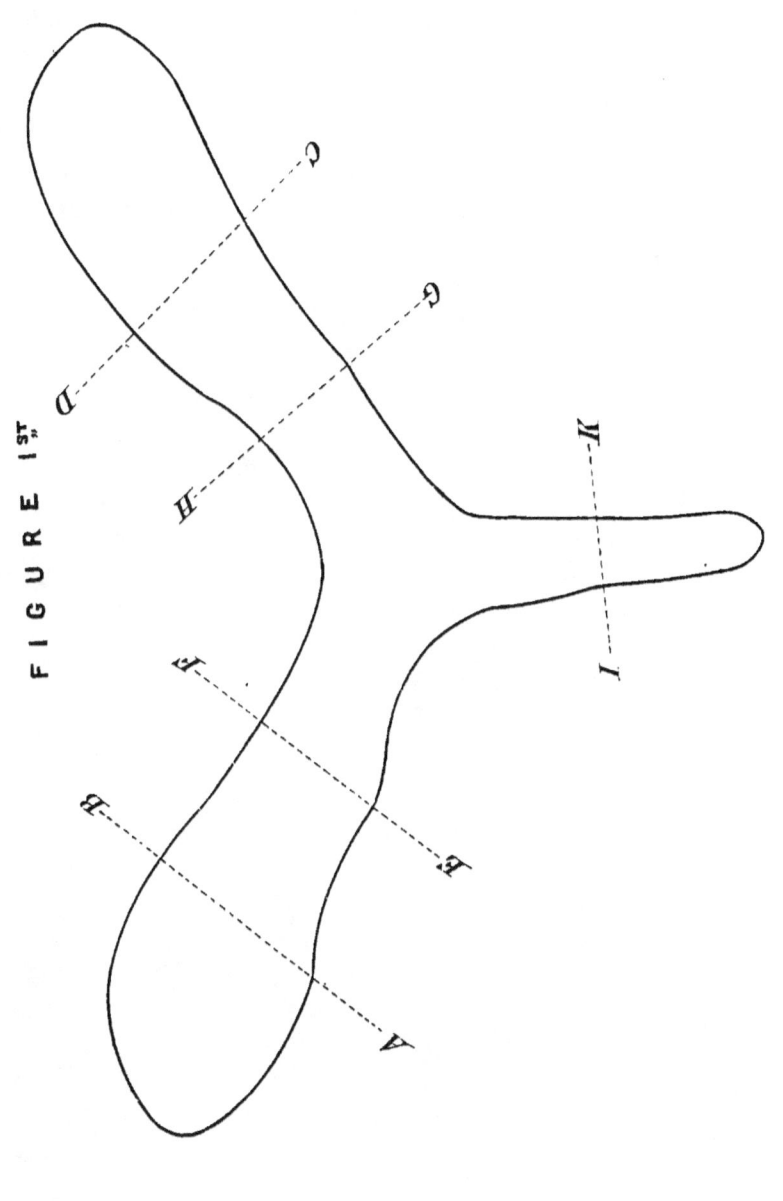

FIGURE 1ST.

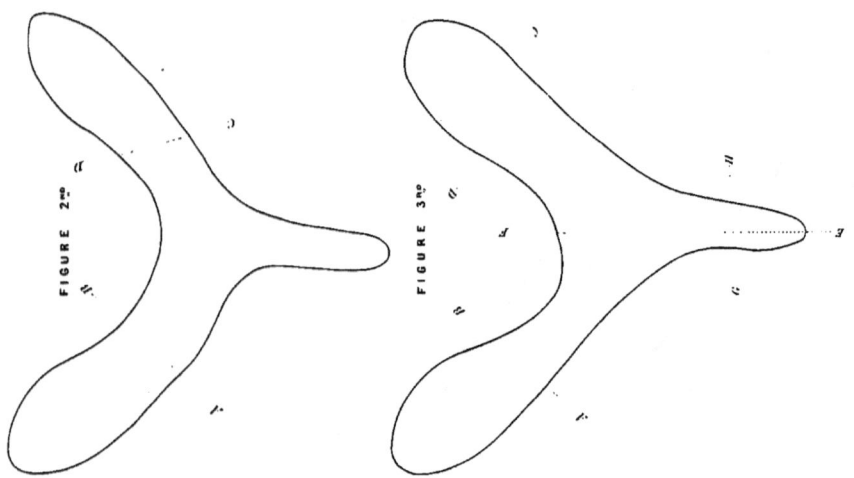

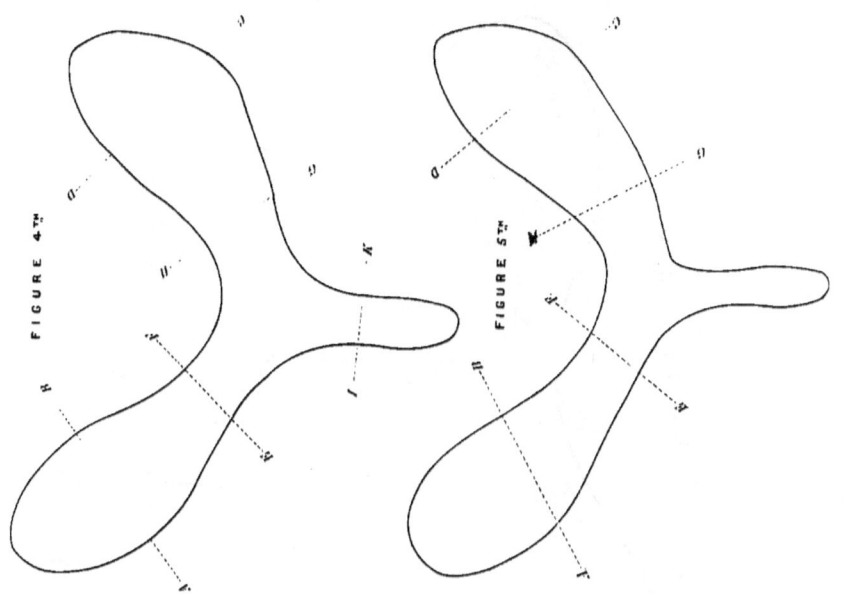

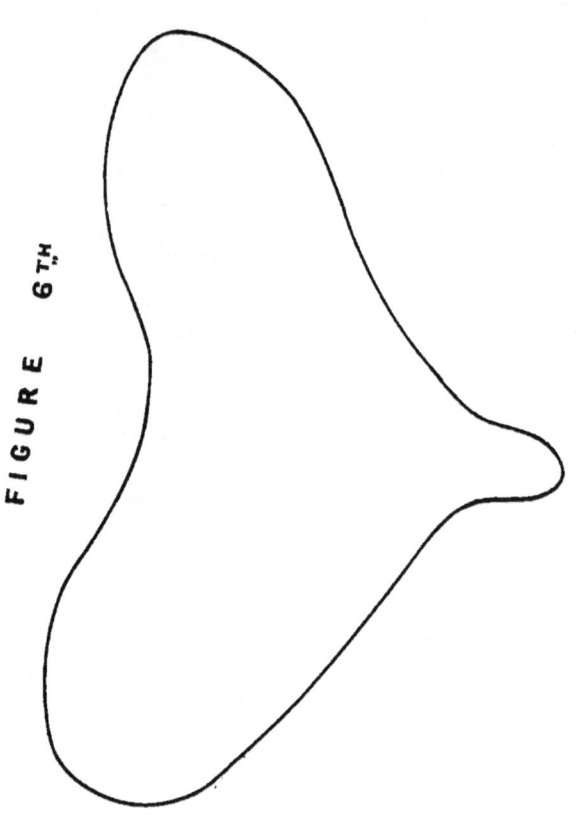

FIGURE 6TH.

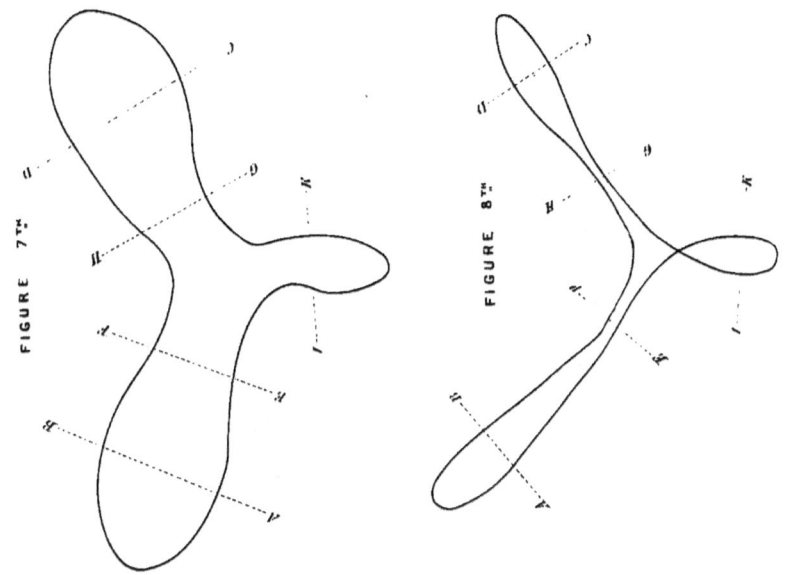

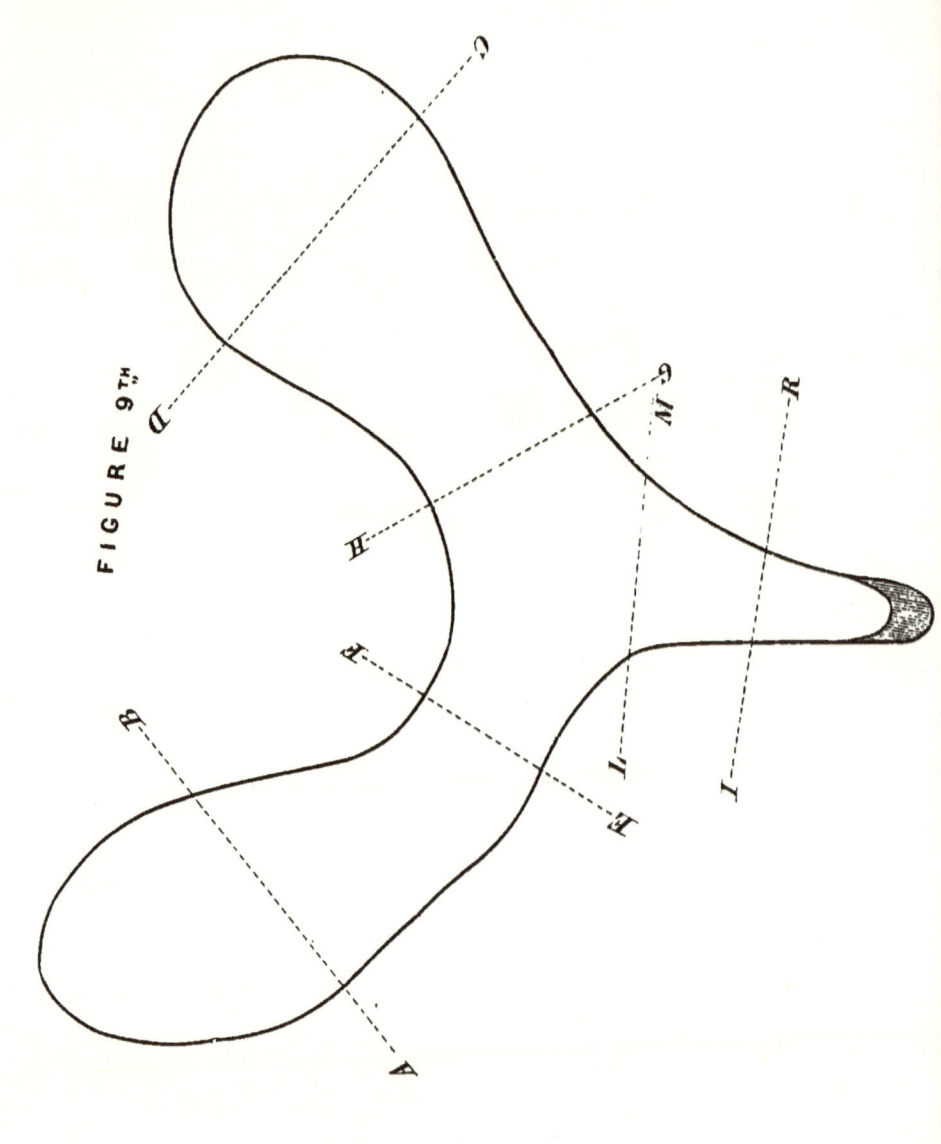

FIGURE 9TH

www.ingramcontent.com/pod-product-compliance
Lightning Source LLC
Chambersburg PA
CBHW032013010726
47493CB00007B/2381